"WHO KILLED HER?"
THEY HAD ASKED AT FIRST.

And now they were asking something else again. Now they were asking, "Who was killed?" They had learned that there were many girls named Annie Boone, and to know who had killed Annie they first had to discover which of the Annies had been killed. The vivacious redhead? The intellectual reader and ballet-goer? The pool-shooter? The divorced wife? The mistress? The mother? The daughter? The social drinker? The drunkard? The girl who talked with a blind boy? Which was Annie? And which Annie had been killed? Or were they all Annie, and had the killer murdered someone who was all things to all men?

KILLER'S CHOICE

BY
Ed McBain

BALLANTINE BOOKS • NEW YORK

The city in these pages is imaginary.
The people, the places are all fictitious.
Only the police routine is based on established investi-
  gatory technique.

CHAPTER 1

THE LIQUOR store reeked.

Shards of glass covered the floor like broken chords from a bop chorus. Long slivers and short slivers, jagged necks of bottles, the round flat bottoms of bottles, glistening, tinkling underfoot so that you waded through a shallow pool of shattered glass. A hand had swept across the shelves, swept in a destructive frenzy. Eight-dollar scotch and twenty-five-cent wine had been spilled to the floor and mingled in the democracy of total destruction. The stench assailed the nostrils the moment you entered the shop. The alcohol spread over the bare wooden floor, sloshed in aromatic puddles underfoot, channeled by the dams and dikes of broken glass.

The girl lay among the glass and the liquid, lay face downward, her mouth partially opened. The girl was a redhead. Her eyes seemed too large for her face because they were bulging in death. The girl had been shot four times in the chest, and her blood still ran, mingling with the alcohol on the floor. Her hair was long, wet and straggly now because her cheek was against the bare wood of the floor, and her hair, her clothes, her body were soaked with alcohol.

It was difficult to talk inside the shop. There wasn't a cop present who didn't enjoy a hooker of booze now and then. But the alcohol fumes inside the shop, despite the fact that the door was open and a mild June breeze was blowing, were overpowering. They caught at the nose, and the throat, and the lungs until breathing them brought on a little dizziness.

Detective Steve Carella was glad to get outside. He en-

5

joyed whiskey, and could knock over a fifth with the best of them. But he could never stand a drunkard breathing in his face, and the liquor store smelled like a convention of drunks all trying to tell the same bad joke simultaneously.

The bad joke was the redhead lying on the floor of the shop. She would have been a bad joke at any time of the year, but especially in June when the world was coming alive, when the month of weddings had mated Spring's exuberance with Summer's warmth. Carella liked being alive, and he was tolerant enough to want to share the experience with everyone. Forced by his occupation to deal with the facts of sudden death, he had still never grown used to the dispassionate façade his colleagues presented. Carella liked to think there was dignity in human beings. They boffed, they drank, they belched, they fought, they swore—but they stood erect.

From somewhere in his memory, probably from a long-forgotten college anthropology course, he dug out the sentence, "Man stands alone—because man alone stands." The anthropological implications were many, but Carella chose to ignore them. He liked to think of man as *standing*. Death knocked a man down. Death stole a man's dignity. A dead man didn't care whether or not his hair was parted. A dead girl didn't worry about whether or not her slip was showing. The postures of death managed to simplify a human being to an angular mound of fleshy rubble. And so looking at what had once been a woman— a woman who smiled prettily, and kissed her lover, and adjusted her stockings, and applied lipstick with utmost feminine care—looking at what had once been warm and alive, Carella felt overwhelming sadness, a sense of tragedy which he could not quite grasp.

He was glad to get outside.

On the sidewalk, the police department held its conference. This was the cocktail party of law enforcement. There were no drinks, and these men did not gather to discuss the latest novel by a twelve-year-old French girl, but there was the same feeling of camaraderie almost, the same easy relationship that comes from knowing men share the same profession.

The two men from Homicide North were called Monoghan and Monroe. Both were huge. Both wore tweed sports jackets over grey flannel slacks.

6

"We don't usually go out on stuff like this," Monoghan said to Carella.

"Not generally," Monroe said.

"The Skipper saves us for tough nuts," Monoghan said.

"The hard ones," Monroe added.

"No crimes of passion."

"Love, hate, like that," Monroe explained.

"Premeditated stuff," Monoghan said.

"Thought out beforehand," Monroe amplified.

"We're his top men," Monoghan said modestly.

"Crackerjacks," Monroe said.

"The 87th Precinct is flattered," Carella said, grinning. He was a tall man wearing a blue worsted suit, a white handkerchief showing at the breast pocket. His shirt was white, and his tie was a blue-and-gold rep, and he talked to the Homicide dicks standing in athletic nonchalance, a man completely at home within the hard, lithe muscularity of his body. His eyes were brown, and his cheekbones were high, and there was a clean-shaved almost-Oriental look to his face, heightened by the secret amusement with which he viewed Monoghan and Monroe.

"The 87th *should* be flattered," Monoghan said.

"Overwhelmed," Monroe added.

"Ecstatic," Carella said.

"Everybody wants to get in the act," Monoghan said.

"Don't misunderstand me," Carella said. "It's just that we appreciate getting Homicide North's top men."

"He's kidding us," Monoghan said.

"Ribbing us," Monroe added.

"He thinks the 87th can do without us."

"He thinks he doesn't need us."

"Who needs us?"

"Like a hole in the head."

"He's telling us to go home."

"He's telling us politely to go to hell."

"Well, frig him," Monoghan said.

Carella grinned, and then his face went serious. He looked into the shop. "What do you make of it?" he asked.

Monoghan and Monroe turned simultaneously. Inside the store, the police photographer leaned closer to the body lying on the alcohol-soaked shards. His flashbulb popped.

"It looks to me," Monoghan said thoughtfully, "like as if somebody went berserk."

CHAPTER 2

MEYER MEYER would miss the bar mìtzvah, of that he was certain.

Naturally, he could not complain. He had arranged with the lieutenant to be off on the day of the bar mitzvah, but the lieutenant had not known there would be a homicide the day before. In the 87th, of course, there was the possibility of a homicide happening *any* day. You just had to plan your bar mitzvahs so that they didn't clash with your homicides.

Not that Meyer Meyer really gave a damn. The child being confirmed was an obnoxious little monster named Irwin, whom the family fondly called Irwin the Vermin. But the child was his wife's sister's son, and that made Meyer his uncle, and he supposed he should have felt some sort of familial affection for the dear lad. Besides, his wife would never let him hear the end of this. Sarah would rant and rave for a week about the big bar mitzvah she missed. His dinners would come from cans. His bridal chamber would not echo to the rhythm of resounding springs. Oh well, *ah zei gei-tus.*

The man sitting opposite Meyer Meyer in the squad room of the 87th Precinct did not know that Meyer was going to miss the confirmation of Irwin the Vermin. He couldn't have cared less. Murder had been done in the man's liquor store, and there was one thing and one thing alone on his mind.

"Four thousand dollars worth of stock!" he shouted. "Who's supposed to pay for that? Me? Am I supposed to take the loss?"

"Would you like the police department to send you a check, Mr. Phelps?" Meyer asked. He asked the question patiently, and with guileless blue eyes, for Meyer Meyer was a very patient man. His father, you see, had considered himself something of a home-grown comedian and had thought it would be sidesplittingly humorous to give his son a given name which would match his surname. The result was Meyer Meyer, a truly hilarious masterpiece, a very funny bit of nomenclature. Meyer happened to be an Orthodox Jew who was raised in a predominantly Gentile neighborhood. If the kids in the streets needed any further provocation for beating him up whenever the opportunity presented itself, Meyer's double-barreled name provided it. He had, over the years, developed an almost supernatural patience concerning the accidents of birth and the vagaries of funny fathers. The patience had left almost no physical scars—except a completely bald head before Meyer had reached the age of thirty. He was now thirty-seven, and he was missing a bar mitzvah, and he leaned across the desk with utmost patience and waited for Mr. Phelps' answer.

"Well, who *is* supposed to pay for it?" Phelps wanted to know. "Me? Who pays for the salary of policemen in this city, if not me? So what do I get in return? Do I get protection? Does four thousand dollars worth of destruction . . . ?"

"A girl was killed," Meyer said patiently.

"Yes, yes, I know," Phelps said. "Do you know how long it's taken me to build that spot? It's not on the main drag, you know, it's not in a brightly lighted area. People come there because of the reputation I've built, and that's the only reason. There are more liquor stores in this precinct than . . ."

"What time did you leave the shop last night, Mr. Phelps?" Meyer asked.

"What difference does it make? Did you see the place? Did you see all those broken bottles? Almost my entire stock! Where was the cop on the beat? How could anyone break all those bottles without attracting . . . ?"

"And fire four shots. Whoever broke the bottles fired four shots, Mr. Phelps."

"Yes, yes, I know. All right, there aren't many apartment buildings in the block, no people to hear. But isn't a cop *supposed* to hear? Where was the cop on the beat? In some damn bar drinking himself silly?"

"He was, as a matter of fact, answering another call."

"What's more important? My stock, or another damn call?"

"Your stock is very important, Mr. Phelps," Meyer said. "Without your stock, the people of this precinct might very well shrivel up and die. The police department never underestimated the value of your stock. But a man was being held up approximately twelve blocks away. A cop can handle only one crime at a time."

"Suppose my store was being held up? What then, huh?"

"Your store wasn't being held up. As I understand it, none of the money in the cash register was touched."

"Thank God I'd only left about fifty dollars for Annie. Just to wind up the night."

"Had Annie worked for you a long time?"

"About a year."

"Would you say . . . ?"

"God, all that stock. It'll cost a fortune to replace."

"What about Annie?" Meyer said, and his patience seemed suddenly to wear very thin.

"Annie?"

"The girl who was killed. The girl who was laying with her broken body and her pretty face in the goddamn remains of your *stock!*"

"Oh. Annie."

"Can we talk about her for a few minutes? Would that be all right with you, Mr. Phelps?"

"Yes, of course. Certainly."

"Annie Boone. Is that her name as you knew it?"

"Yes."

"And she worked for you for a year, is that right?"

"Yes. Just about a year."

"Was she married?"

"Yes."

"Are you sure?"

"Yes."

"We have her listed as divorced."

"Oh. Well, yes, I suppose she was."

"One child, is that right? Left the child with her mother when she was working."

"Yes, that's right. A boy, I believe."

"No," Meyer said. "A girl."

"Oh. Was it a girl? Well, then I suppose so."

"Thirty-two years old, right, Mr. Phelps?"

"Yes. Thirty-two or thirty-three."

"Are you married, Mr. Phelps?"

"Me?"

"Yes."

"I thought we were talking about Annie."

"We were. Now we're talking about you."

"Yes, I'm married."

"How long?"

"Fourteen years."

"Children?"

"No. No children."

"How old are you, Mr. Phelps?"

"I'm forty-one."

"Get along?"

"What?"

"Do you get along with your wife?"

"What!"

"I said," Meyer repeated patiently, "do you get along with your wife?"

"Well, of course I do! What the hell kind of a question is that to ask?"

"Don't get excited, Mr. Phelps. Lots of men don't."

"Well, I do! And I don't see how this line of questioning is going to find the person who wrecked my store."

"We're primarily interested in the person who did murder, Mr. Phelps."

"Then I suppose I should be delighted that Annie was killed. Otherwise the police would be happy to pass off the wreckage as just one of those unfortunate breaks."

"I think you're oversimplifying it, Mr. Phelps," Meyer said. He looked up suddenly. "Do you own a revolver?"

"What?"

"A revolver? A pistol? A gun?"

"No."

"Are you sure?"

"Of course, I'm sure."

"We can check, you know."

"Of course I know you can ch . . ." Phelps stopped talking. Slow recognition crossed his face. He studied Meyer, and then a scowl brought his eyebrows into sharp angry wings. "What are you saying?"

"Hmh?" Meyer asked.

"I'm not a suspect, am I? You're not saying that I'm a suspect?"

Meyer nodded sadly. "Yes, Mr. Phelps," he said. "I'm afraid you are."

The man in Lieutenant Byrnes' office was six feet two inches tall, and he weighed one hundred and ninety pounds. He had blue eyes and a square jaw with a cleft chin. His hair was red, except for a streak over his left temple where he had once been knifed and where the hair had curiously grown in white after the wound had healed. He had a straight unbroken nose, and a good mouth with a wide lower lip. There was something of arrogance on his face, as if he did not approve of the lieutenant, or of Carella who stood alongside the lieutenant's desk, or even in fact of the lieutenant's office.

"Steve," Byrnes said, "this is . . . ah . . ." Byrnes consulted the sheet of paper in his right hand. ". . . ah . . . Cotton Hawes." He looked at the redhead curiously. "Is that right? Cotton Hawes?"

"Yes, sir. Cotton."

Byrnes cleared his throat. "Cotton Hawes," he said again, and he stole a somewhat surreptitious glance at Carella, and then was silent for a moment as if he were allowing the name to penetrate the layers of his mind. "Detective 2nd/Grade," he said at last, "be working out of this squad from now on. Transfer from the 30th."

Carella nodded.

"This is Steve Carella," Byrnes said.

Carella extended his hand. "Glad to know you."

"Carella," Hawes answered, and he took Carella's hand in a firm grip. There were red hairs curling on the backs of Hawes' hands, and the hands were big. But Carella noticed that he did not try a bonecrusher handshake, the way some big men did. He gripped Carella's hand firmly and briefly, and then let it drop.

"I thought Steve might show you the ropes," Byrnes said.

"How did you mean, sir?" Hawes asked.

"Huh?"

"How did you mean, sir?"

"Show you around," Byrnes said. "The squad, and the

house, and maybe the streets. Won't hurt to get to know the precinct."

"No, sir."

"In the meantime, Cotton . . ." Byrnes paused. "Is . . . ah . . . that what people call you? Cotton?"

"Yes, sir. Cotton."

"Well . . . ah . . . in the meantime, Hawes, we're happy to have you aboard. You won't find the 87th to be a garden spot, not after working in the 30th. But it's not such a bad dump."

"It's pretty bad," Carella said.

"Well, yes, as a matter of fact, it's pretty bad. But you'll get used to it. Or it'll get used to you. It's hard to tell which around here."

"I'm sure I'll get into the swing of things, sir," Hawes said.

"Oh, no question, no question." Byrnes paused again. "Well, unless there was anything else . . ." He paused. He felt exceptionally awkward in the presence of Hawes, and he did not know why. "You might show him around, Steve," he concluded.

"Yes, sir," Carella said, and he led Hawes to the door which opened on the Detective Squad Room. "I guess the layout is pretty much the same all over the city," he said when they were outside.

"More or less," Hawes said.

"Cotton," Carella said. "That's an unusual name."

"My father was intrigued with the Puritan priest."

"Huh?"

"Cotton Mather. Figured him to be one of the great colonists. It could have been worse."

"How so?"

"He might have named me Increase."

"Yeah," Carella said, smiling. "Well, this is the squad room. Desks, windows—bulletin board there has the wanted posters and any notices we don't know what to do with. Filing cabinets are over there on your right. The usual stuff. Lousy File, Wanted cards, Arrests, Stolen Goods, hell, it must have been the same in your squad."

"Sure," Hawes said.

"We've got a file on lost bicycles," Carella said. "Maybe you didn't have that."

"No, we didn't."

"Helps every now and then. Lots of kids in this precinct."

"Um-huh."

"Only free desk we've got is the one by the window. We use it as a junk collector. You'll find everything in it but your mother-in-law."

"I'm not married," Hawes said.

"Oh. Well. Anyway, we can clean it out, and you can use it. If in case you ever do get married." He smiled, but Hawes did not return the smile. "Well . . . uh . . ." Carella paused, thinking. His eye lighted on Meyer Meyer and he quickly said, "Meyer!" and Meyer looked up from his typewriter. Carella steered Hawes over to the desk.

"Meyer, meet Cotton Hawes, just assigned to the squad. Cotton, this is Meyer Meyer."

Meyer extended his hand and started to say, "How do you . . ." and then he cut himself short and asked, "How was that again?"

"Cotton Hawes," Hawes said.

"Oh. How do you do?" He took Hawes' hand.

"Meyer is the only man in the world with two first names," Carella said. "Or two last names, depending how you look at it."

"With the exception of Harry James," Hawes said.

"Huh? Harry . . . ? Oh, Harry James. Two first names. Yes. Yes," Carella said. He cleared his throat. "What are you working on, Harry . . . uh . . . Meyer?"

"This liquor store kill," Meyer said. "I just interrogated the owner. I'm going to miss my bar mitzvah."

"How come?"

"Time I get finished typing up this report." He looked at his watch.

"Hell, it shouldn't take that long," Carella said.

"Don't rush me," Meyer said. "I think maybe I *want* to miss that lousy bar mitzvah."

"Well, you'll be seeing Cotton around," Carella said. "I know you'll make him at home."

"Sure," Meyer said indifferently, and he went back to typing up his report.

"Through the railing here is the corridor leading to the locker room. On your left is the Clerical Office, the latrine . . . you an Army man?"

14

"Navy," Hawes said.

"Oh. Did they teach you any judo?"

"A little."

"We've got a whiz working with us. Fellow named Hal Willis. You'll have a lot to talk about."

"Will we?" Hawes said.

"Just don't shake hands with him," Carella said jokingly. "He can have you on your back in three seconds."

"Can he?" Hawes asked drily.

"Well, he . . ." Carella cleared his throat again. "Interrogation is at the end of the hall, if you feel you need privacy. We generally question suspects in the squad room. The Skipper doesn't like rough stuff."

"I never saw a prisoner maltreated all the while I was with the 30th squad," Hawes said.

"Well, that's a pretty good neighborhood, isn't it?" Carella said.

"We had our share of crime," Hawes said.

"Sure, I didn't doubt . . ." Carella let the sentence trail. "Locker room is right there at the end of the hall. Steps here lead to the desk downstairs and the Waldorf Suite at the back of the building."

"The *what?*"

"Detention cells."

"Oh."

"Come on down, I'll introduce you to the desk sergeant. Then we can take a walk around the precinct if you like."

"Whatever you say," Hawes said.

"Oh, it's my pleasure," Carella answered, in his first display of sarcasm all day. Hawes chose to ignore the thrust. Together they walked down the steps to the ground floor, silently.

CHAPTER 3

THE WOMAN who sat in the small living room was fifty-four years old, and had once had hair as bright and as red as her daughter's. The hair was now streaked with grey, but it did not give the impression of red hair turning. Instead, and paradoxically, it looked like iron grey hair streaked with rust.

The woman's face was streaked with tears. The tears had destroyed the mascara around her eyes, sent it trickling down her cheeks, and was now demolishing the pancake makeup on her face. The woman was no beauty to begin with, and sorrow had stabbed at her eyes and was now trickling down her face, disintegrating the mask of beauty she donned for the world, the mask of beauty which news of death was ripping away piece by crumbling piece.

Detective Bert Kling sat opposite her and watched her. He did not like questioning women, and he did not like questioning women who cried. In homicides, in suicides, the women always cried. He felt uncomfortable in the presence of a crying woman. He was a new detective, and a very young detective, and he had not yet acquired either the sympathy or the *savoir faire* of a man like Carella. And so the woman's tears dissolved more than her carefully madeup face. They also dissolved the external façade of one Bert Kling, so that he sat like a dumbstruck schoolboy, unable to utter a syllable.

The living room was furnished comfortably and taste-fully. The furniture was not expensive, but it boasted clean modern lines without the cumbersome heavy look of furniture that hugs the floor, furniture that crowds a small apartment. The upholstery was light and gay, too, in sharp contrast to the woman who sat on the couch daubing at her

16

brown-streaked eyes and face. There was a huge photograph of a vivacious redhead on the wall over the couch. The redhead had been photographed in a field of waving wheat, her head thrown back to the skies, the red hair streaming over her shoulders. There was pure soaring joy on her face, and Kling thought back to the face he had seen pressed against the wooden floor of the liquor shop, and he thought fleetingly of life and death, of joy and sorrow.

"Annie," the woman said, following his glance.

"Yes," Kling answered.

"That was taken seven years ago. On her honeymoon. They went to his father's farm in Indiana. Stayed a month. She was happy."

"Ted Boone," Kling said. "That was her husband's name, wasn't it?"

"Theodore, yes. I always called him Theodore. He was a nice boy. A photographer, you know. He took that picture. Blew it up from a small Kodachrome. He's very talented."

"Do you have any idea why they got divorced?"

"Yes."

"Why?"

"He outgrew my daughter." The words were delivered flatly with no emotion, a flat statement of fact.

"How do you mean, Mrs. Travail?"

"He just outgrew her. Annie wasn't very bright. She's . . . she was my daughter, but not very bright. Always full of fun, though, and spirit, do you know the kind of girl I mean? Dancing, and laughing, and well . . . gay. And a boy like Theodore found her attractive. A lot of boys found her attractive. After a while, though . . ." Mrs. Travail paused, and there was grief on her face still, but she was not thinking of death now. She was trying to vocalize things she had probably never said to anyone, things a mother doesn't say even to her daughter, except when the stranger Death intrudes, and then there are no secrets, then there are no feelings to protect, no pride to fear injuring. "Theodore grew. Not only with his photography. I knew he would grow with that. But here." She tapped her temple. "He wanted more. He was hungry for learning, and experience, and stimulation. Annie couldn't give it to him. He asked her for a divorce."

"Did she grant it?"

"Yes. She didn't like the idea. They'd had Monica by then—the girl, my granddaughter—and a woman gets afraid, Mr. Kling. A woman who's been married for five years, living with a man, becoming a wife and a mother, she gets afraid. She doesn't know the . . . the game anymore. The game the single ones play. It isn't easy to think you'll have to get back into the game again." Mrs. Travail sighed. "But she let him go. You can't hold an eagle if you're a sparrow, Mr. Kling. You just can't."

"Did they part amicably?"

"Does any divorced couple ever part amicably?"

"Well, I . . ."

"Oh, yes, yes, very modern about it. Friends. And, of course, he visited Monica. But it's hard, Mr. Kling, for two people who have known each other intimately, who have known each other's desires and thoughts and dreams, to suddenly part and pretend they are strangers. It's . . . you resent someone who knows you too well. You have asked him to no longer share, and you resent the fact that he once shared."

"I suppose that's true. But there was never any open breach? On his visits, I mean. They didn't argue or anything?"

"Theodore is not a killer," Mrs. Travail said flatly.

"We have to consider every angle, Mrs. Travail."

"I know that. My daughter was murdered, Mr. Kling. She was not a very bright girl, but you mustn't think I didn't care for her deeply. I did. Deeply. And I *want* the police to consider every angle. But Theodore is not a killer. He is a creator. Creators do not destroy."

"I see." Kling sighed. He knew they would have to question Boone, anyway, creator, destroyer, or both. He had learned, however, that one can explain police technique only so far, and then only if one is in a generous mood. The best technique of explaining police technique, he had discovered, was not to explain it at all. Listen, observe, remember, take suggestions. And then go about the job the way it had to be done.

"She was divorced when?"

"Two years ago."

"In this city?"

18

"No. There was no adultery. Theodore lived by the rules as long as there was a contact."

"I see. Did your daughter go to Reno?"

"Las Vegas." Mrs. Travail paused. "Theodore paid for it."

"And the child?"

"Monica stayed with me while Annie went west."

"Do you have any other children, Mrs. Travail? Did Annie have a brother or sister?"

"A brother."

"Where can I reach him, Mrs. Travail?"

"He's dead."

"Oh. Oh, I'm sorry."

"He was killed in the Second World War. He was a gunner on a navy plane."

"I'm sorry."

"He was nineteen when he died. First I lost my husband, and then my only son. All I . . . all I had was Annie. And Theodore, of course, later. Then . . . then Theodore was gone and now . . . now I'm alone again. Except for the child. I have the child. I have the little girl."

"Yes," Kling said.

"But a woman needs . . . needs men around her, Mr. Kling. A woman needs men."

"Yes."

"Theodore was a good man."

"Your daughter, Mrs. Travail," Kling reminded.

"Yes?"

"Had she been seeing any men lately?"

"Yes."

"Who?"

"Several."

"Do you want to give me their names?"

"Yes, surely. She was seeing a man named Arthur Cordis. She saw him . . . oh . . . every other week perhaps."

"He called for her here?"

"Yes."

"Would you know where he lives?"

"In Isola some place. I don't know the address. He's a bank teller."

"Who else?"

"Frank Abelson."

"How often did she see him?"

"On and off. None of them really meant anything to her. They were just . . . companions, I suppose you would call them."

"And he lives?"

"Isola, too."

"Who else?"

"A boy named Jamie."

"Jamie what?"

"I don't know. I only spoke to him on the phone. He'd never been here."

"But your daughter was seeing him?"

"Yes. They met somewhere. I don't know why he never called for her."

"You're sure about this?"

"Yes. He called her on the phone often. She spoke of him, too. She said he was a very nice boy."

"How about girl friends, Mrs. Travail?"

"Oh, Annie had quite a few. Do you want me to name them all? Wouldn't it be easier if you took her address book?"

"Do you have it?"

"Yes."

"When I leave, then."

"Certainly."

"Now, let's see," King said, consulting his notes. "She had been working at the liquor store for a year, is that right?"

"Yes. She had another job after the divorce. When she left that, she went to work for Mr. Phelps."

"Did she get on well with Mr. Phelps?"

"Oh, yes. He was a very considerate man."

"How?"

"As an employer, I mean. Very considerate."

"Mmm," Kling said, thinking of what Meyer had told him of Phelps. "How do you mean, considerate?"

"Well, she always spoke kindly of him. And once, I remember, she was home sick with a virus and he sent her flowers."

"Oh?"

"Yes. A dozen red roses."

"Isn't that a little unusual?"

"Women like flowers," Mrs. Travail said. "Annie was a good worker."

"Where did she work last, Mrs. Travail? Before the liquor store?"

"A furniture house. Herman Dodson, Inc."

"Would you happen to know what she did there?"

"She was a saleslady."

"Why did she leave?"

"I don't know. We never discussed it. I think the salary wasn't high enough."

"How did she get the job at the liquor store?"

"I don't know. She just heard of it somehow."

"I see."

"Do you have any idea who did this, Mr. Kling?"

"No. Not yet. We're just beginning, Mrs. Travail. It sometimes takes a long while. You can understand that."

"Yes, certainly. Of course, I can understand that."

"Do you want to get that address book for me?"

"Yes, certainly. She kept it in her room, on her desk. I'll get it for you."

Mrs. Travail wiped at her mascara-running eyes and then left the room. Kling sat. When the front door opened, he turned automatically to face it, and his hand edged slightly toward the .38 Detective's Special in his shoulder holster. When he saw who was in the doorframe, his hand relaxed.

"Hello," the girl said.

"Hello, Monica," he answered, smiling.

The girl looked puzzled. She had bright red hair braided into pigtails. She wore a plaid skirt with shoulder straps and a white blouse. Her legs were straight and her teeth were good, and she looked at Kling with the wide-eyed candor of a child. "How do you know my name?"

"I just do," Kling said.

"Is Granma home?"

"Yes. She went to get something for me. From Mommy's room."

"I don't call her Mommy," Monica confided. "Granma doesn't like that. I call her Mother."

"Don't you call Granma Grandmother?"

"Only when she's around," Monica said, giggling and then stifling the laugh with a cupped hand. "What's your name?"

21

"Bert."

"Are you one of Mother's boy friends?"

"No," Kling said.

"What are you?"

"I'm a cop."

"Really?" Monica asked, her eyes wider. "Like on *Dragnet?*"

"Better than *Dragnet,*" Kling said, modestly.

"Do you have a gun?"

"Sure."

"Could I see it?"

Kling unholstered the .38 and checked the safety to make sure it was on. Monica came close to the gun, but Kling did not let it out of his hand.

"Is it real?"

"Certainly," Kling said.

"Where'd you get it?"

"In a box of Rice Krispies."

"You didn't!"

"No, not really. How old are you, Monica?"

"Five. I'll be six soon."

Kling holstered the gun. "Are you just getting home from school?"

"Yes. I only go half a day because I'm still in kindergarten. Next term I'll be in the first grade. Then I'll go all day, and I'll have books. I never met a cop before."

"I never met a little girl in kindergarten before."

"Oh, we're nothing special."

"Everybody's something special, Monica."

"Why are you here?"

"Oh, just a routine check."

"That's what they say on *Dragnet.*"

"Well, they're right."

"A routine check on what?" Monica asked.

"On five-year-old girls who are in kindergarten."

"Why?" Monica asked seriously. "Did one *do* something?"

Kling burst out laughing. "No, honey," he said. "I was only joking."

"Then why are you here?"

"Routine," he said.

This was not his job. Telling a five-year-old button that her mother had been shot dead was not his job. He had sworn the oath, and he believed he was a good cop, but this was action far above and beyond the call of duty, and maybe Carella could take a five-year-old redhead on his knee and gently and patiently explain to her that her mother had been shot four times in the chest, but Kling could not. Not yet. Maybe years from now. But not yet.

"What kind of routine?" Monica asked persistently, and Kling was extremely grateful for Mrs. Travail who entered the room at that moment.

"Here's the . . . oh!" She saw Monica and her eyes fled instantly to Kling's face. "You didn't . . ."

"No," Kling said.

"Didn't what?" Monica asked.

"Nothing, darling. Have you met Detective Kling?"

"His name is Bert," Monica said.

"Then you *have* met."

"Sure. He's here on routine."

"Yes," Mrs. Travail said. "How was school today, darling?"

"Oh, the same old jazz," Monica said.

"Monica!"

Kling tried to suppress his smile.

"Why don't you go to your room, Monica?" Mrs. Travail said. "Mr. Kling and I have some business to finish."

"Sure," Monica said. She turned to Kling and said, "Where's Frank Smith?"

"Out on a 365 W," Kling said, and Monica laughed in delight.

"Will you call me when you're through, Grandmother?" she said politely.

"Yes, dear."

"Goodbye, Mr. Kling. I hope you find her."

"I hope so, too."

Monica left the room. Mrs. Travail waited for her to leave and then said, "She wasn't referring to . . ."

"No. A private joke between us."

"Do you think a woman *might* have killed my daughter?"

"It's possible."

"Here's the address book. All her girl friends are in it." She handed Kling the book.

"Thank you, Mrs. Travail," he said. "And thank you for your cooperation."

At the door, Mrs. Travail said, "You *are* going to visit Theodore, aren't you?"

"Yes," Kling said. "We are."

"He didn't do it," Mrs. Travail said evenly. "Good day, Mr. Kling."

CHAPTER 4

HERMAN DODSON, INC.

Fine Furnitures

June 12, 1957

Detective Bertram Kling
87th Detective Squad
457 Parkside
Isola

Dear Detective Kling:

In answer to your telephone query of yesterday, I asked our Personnel Manager to consult our files on the employment of Anne Carolyn Boone. He has done so, and given me a full report, and I pass this on to you for whatever it is worth.

Miss Boone answered a blind advertisement in a local daily run on Sunday, March 13, 1955. The advertisement read:

WANTED

Experienced saleswoman for established quality furniture store. Salary plus commission. Call PAtrick 3-7021.

Miss Boone called and was granted an interview. As it turned out, she had never had any experience selling furniture, and our Personnel Manager was somewhat hesitant about hiring her. But, as you probably know, she had recently been divorced, and she was a rather attractive girl with

25

a warm-spirited personality. We felt we could use her personality to good advantage in our modern furniture department, and we employed her for a trial period of six months. Her starting salary was $45.00 per week, plus commissions, of course, with the understanding that she would be given an increase of $5.00 per week at the end of the six-month period, should her employment prove satisfactory.

As it turned out, our judgment was not at all inaccurate. Miss Boone was a fine worker and a good saleswoman. She was well-liked by every employee on the sixth floor (Modern Furniture, Lamps, Etc.) and was regarded as both capable and enthusiastic by the floor manager.

We were, indeed, most distressed to have her leave us last year. We understand, though, that she had a job offering a much higher salary, and we certainly would not stand in the way of opportunity.

I can assure you, Detective Kling, that we learned of her death with great sorrow here at Herman Dodson. Miss Boone was a fine woman and a pleasure to know. She was getting over a most trying experience in her personal life, but she never allowed her private troubles to interfere in any way with her relations with fellow employees or with customers of the store.

I wish you the greatest success in your endeavors to apprehend her murderer. If I can be of any further assistance, please do not hesitate to call.

My very best wishes,
        Sincerely,

        Ralph Dodson

        Ralph Dodson
        for HERMAN DODSON, INC.

RD:eh

Kling studied the letter from Ralph Dodson, and then wondered why anyone had killed Anne Carolyn Boone and then destroyed a liquor store to boot. It did not seem to make much sense. Shrugging, he pulled the Isola telephone directory to him, thumbed it open, and began leafing through the B's. He found a listing for *Theodore Boone, phtgrphr* at 495 Hall Avenue. He asked the desk sergeant for a line, and then dialed the number. The phone was picked up instantly.

"Theodore Boone, good morning," a cheery voice chirped.

"Mr. Boone, please," Kling said.

"Who's calling, please?"

"Detective Bert Kling of the 87th Detective Squad."

"Oh," the voice said.

"Is he in?"

"I don't know, sir. Just one moment, and I'll see."

Kling waited. While he waited, he drew a picture of a man with a beard, and he put eyeglasses on the man and then a spotted sports shirt. He was ready to hang up and dial again when the voice came onto the line. It was a deep voice, a good voice, a real voice.

"Hello?"

"Mr. Boone?"

"Yes?"

"Detective Kling, 87th Squad."

"I've been expecting this," Boone said. "It's about Annie, isn't it?"

"Yes, sir."

"How can I help?" Boone wanted to know.

"I'd like to talk to you, Mr. Boone. Can I see you sometime this afternoon?"

"Yes. Just a moment, let me check my appointments." There was a pause on the line. "Three o'clock all right?"

"Fine."

"I can squeeze you in, I think. I don't mean to sound rude, Mr. Kling, but I've got a session scheduled for three-thirty."

"Not at all," Kling said. "I'll be there on the button."

"Fine. Look forward to seeing you," and Boone hung up.

Kling held the dead phone just a moment, and then he replaced it on its cradle. He looked at his watch, walked over to where Meyer Meyer was typing at the next desk and said, "Come on, coolie. It's lunch time."

"Already?" Meyer asked, looking up at the wall clock.

"My God!" he complained. "All we ever do around here is *fress. Fress, fress, fress.*"

But he put on his jacket, and at the greasy spoon in one of the sidestreets near the squad, he ate Kling clear under the table—which was no small feat.

Peter Kronig was, like Cotton Hawes, a transfer. Unlike Hawes, he was not a transfer from one precinct to another. He had once been a police photographer but he had been transferred to the Police Laboratory to study under Lieutenant Sam Grossman who was his immediate superior and who probably ran the best damn lab in the United States. Actually, Kronig had worked pretty closely with the lab even when he'd been a photographer. It was, in fact, his deep interest in laboratory work which had accounted for the transfer. Lab technicians were difficult enough to come by, God knew, and when Grossman saw a man with real interest, he grabbed him—but fast.

Kronig had been grabbed, and he was learning that there was a good deal more to scientific detection than the mere developing of negatives or emulsification of prints. In the orderly white room which stretched for almost the entire first floor of the headquarters building on High Street downtown, he was learning that scientific detection meant dealing with detectives who were interested in homicide. He did not mind dealing with Steve Carella so much. Carella was a cop whom he'd seen around when he was still shooting stiffs. Carella was always good for a laugh, and Carella also happened to be a good cop who asked pertinent questions and who didn't let very much of importance get by him. But this fellow Hawes—*Cotton* Hawes, Jesus!—was showing every indication of being a difficult fellow to keep up with. Kronig did not like to run intellectual races. Hawes was as sharp as a plate glass splinter, and as cold as a plate of spumoni. It was the coldness that got Kronig. Even wearing his Detective's 3rd/Grade shield, he'd have hated to meet Hawes in a dark alley.

"We can, as you know, determine the make of an unknown firearm as long as we have the bullet which was fired from it," he said.

"That's why we're here," Hawes said drily.

"Yes," Kronig said. "Well, we examine the grooves on

28

the bullet, the right- or left-hand direction of the grooves, their number, their width, and degree of twist of the spiral. That's what we do."

"What about the gun that murdered Anne Boone?" Hawes asked.

"Yes. I was getting to that."

"When?" Hawes asked. Carella glanced at him, but Hawes did not glance back.

"A land," Kronig went on, slightly ruffled, "is the smooth surface between the spiral grooves in the pistol barrel. To make things simpler, most pistol barrels have an even number of grooves. For example, there are only eight automatics . . ."

"Eight automatics," Hawes concluded, "which have five lands. What about the murder weapon?"

"I was getting to that," Kronig said. "Most pistols in the .25 calibre group have six lands. If we have two pistols with the same number of lands, we can further differentiate between them by the direction of twist. To the left or to the right, do you understand?"

"It's perfectly clear," Hawes said.

"Hardly any automatics have a left twist," Kronig said.

"There are a few," Hawes answered. "Spanish .25's and .32's have a left twist."

"Yes. Yes. And the Bayard and Colt .25 have a left twist."

"Why are you hitting .25's so hard?" Carella asked.

"Because the sample bullet we examined had six lands. The twist was sixteen inches left. The groove diameter was .251 inches."

"Get to it," Hawes said.

"Well," Kronig said, sighing, "we went to our charts. We looked up grooves, direction of twist, twist in inches, groove diameter, and we came up with the make and calibre of the gun that fired that bullet."

"Which was?"

"A Colt .25 automatic."

"Fill us in, Pete," Carella said.

"Not much to tell. You know .25's. A small gun. Weighs thirteen ounces and has an overall length of four and a half inches. The barrel length is two inches. Magazine capacity, six cartridges. You find them in either blued or nickeled finishes. They've got pearl, ivory, or walnut stocks. They shoot like bastards, and they can kill as dead as a .45."

"A small gun," Carella said.

"And a light one," Hawes added. "Light enough for a man to keep in his side pocket. Light enough for a woman to carry in her purse."

"Not a woman's gun especially, is it, Pete?" Carella asked.

"Not necessarily, Steve," Kronig said. "It could be, but not necessarily. I'd say it's six of one and a half-dozen of the other. Not like a .45. You know, not many women will lug a .45."

"Either a man or a woman," Carella said dismally.

"Mmm," Kronig said, nodding. He grinned at Carella and added, "We've certainly narrowed it down for you, huh?"

In the street outside the headquarters building, Carella said, "Deal much with the lab before, Hawes?"

"A little," Hawes said.

"What was it? Didn't you take to Pete?"

"He was fine. Why?"

"You seemed p.o.'d about something."

"Only his deadly lecture on elementary ballistics," Hawes said.

"That's his job."

"His job was to tell us what make and calibre gun killed Anne Boone. I'm not interested in the processes which lead to his conclusions. Our job is to get a murderer, not listen to a glorified report on laboratory technique."

"It doesn't hurt to know these things," Carella said.

"Why? Do you plan on becoming a lab cop?"

"Nope. But if you can appreciate another man's job, you won't ask the impossible of him."

"That's a generous attitude," Hawes said. "I like to do things fast."

"Sometimes you can't handle homicides fast. We now know that a .25 was used. That's not such a popular calibre. The thieves we deal with seem to favor .32's and .38's. Was it that way at the 30th?"

"Just about."

"So we've got something to look for in the M.O. file.

30

Maybe Pete gave you a lecture, but I didn't mind it. I sort of enjoyed it."

"To each his own," Hawes said flatly.

"Sure. You handle many homicide cases before your transfer, Hawes?"

"Not many."

"Not many?"

"We didn't have many homicides at the 30th."

"No?"

"No."

"How many?"

"What are you getting at, Carella?"

"I'm just curious."

"I'm 'way ahead of you."

"Are you?"

"Yes. You know damn well what kind of a precinct the 30th was. Rich people. Big, fancy apartment houses with doormen. Burglary was our most frequent crime. And street stickups. And attempted and realized suicides. And some high-class prostitution. But not many homicides."

"How many?"

"I won't count the ones where a burglar panicked and killed, and where we grabbed him almost at the scene. I'll only count the real homicides. Where we had to work."

"Sure," Carella said. "How many?"

"Six."

"A week?"

"No."

"What then? A month?"

"I worked out of the 30th squad for four years. We had six homicides in all that time."

"What?"

"Yeah."

"How many of those did you work on?"

"None."

"Oh," Carella said, smiling.

"Did you prove your point?"

"Which point?"

"That I don't know my ass from my elbow?"

"I wasn't trying to prove anything."

"I don't know homicide, that's true. It was always my impression that killings were left to Homicide North or Homicide South."

"If we gave all the 87th's homicides to the Homicide Squads, they wouldn't have enough dicks to go around."

"Okay. I don't know homicide. Are we agreed?"

"We're agreed. What else don't you know?"

"I don't know the 87th Precinct."

"Granted."

"I don't know you, either."

"Stephen Louis Carella, Detective 2nd/Grade, thirty-four years old, been a cop since I was twenty-one. I'm married to a girl named Teddy who's a deaf mute. We're very happy. I like my job. I've worked on forty-one homicide cases, and just about every other type of crime being committed in this city. I made two big mistakes in my lifetime. I jumped on a hand grenade in Italy, and I got myself shot last Christmas. I survived both times, and I won't make the same mistakes again. End of deposition."

"That's it, huh?"

"In a nutshell."

"You're a college man, aren't you?"

"Two and a half years. Chaucer finally threw me."

"You were medically discharged from the Army, right?"

"Yes. How'd . . ."

"If you've been a cop since you're twenty-one, and if you went to college for two and a half years, that doesn't leave much time for the Army. What'd you do? Graduate high school at seventeen, go to school for a year, get drafted, get wounded, get medically discharged, and then go back to school for a year and a half before you joined the force?"

"You're reading it right down the line," Carella said, somewhat amazed.

"Okay. I guess I now know Detective Steve Carella."

"I guess so. How about Detective Cotton Hawes?"

"There's not much to know," Hawes said.

"Tell it."

"It bores me."

"The way Pete Kronig in the lab bored you."

"In a way, yes."

"I'll give you some advice, Hawes."

"What's that?"

"I'm not the best cop in the world," Carella said. "I just try to do my job, that's all. But I've worked on homicides, and I know my job is made a whole lot easier because of Sam Grossman and his technicians. Sometimes the lab isn't worth a damn. Sometimes a case is all legwork and stool pigeons and personal mathematics. But there are times when the lab does everything but go out to make the pinch. When a lab cop talks, I listen. I listen hard."

"You're saying?" Hawes asked.

"I'm saying you've got ears, too," Carella said. "Shall we go get some coffee?"

CHAPTER 5

495 HALL AVENUE was a sumptuous building with a wide entrance lobby and fourteen elevators. It rested in the heart of the publishing section, flanked on either side by the high-class department stores which lined the street.

Kling felt as if he'd died and gone to heaven.

It was a distinct pleasure to get away from the 87th. There was a nice feeling to midtown Isola, a feeling he had almost forgotten. He could remember Christmas shopping with Claire, his fiancée, but this was June and Christmas seemed as if it had happened in 1776. It was good to be back on Hall Avenue, good to see men carrying brief cases and going about clean jobs, good to see girls in tailored suits or skirts and blouses, clean-scrubbed girls hurrying to their offices, or hurrying to do their shopping. This was the nicest part of the city, he felt, the part that really *felt* like it, that really made you think you were in a giant metropolis.

The weather, too, was ideal. Summer had not yet begun its onslaught. Spring had not yet left the air. It was mild and balmy, a day for taking off your shoes and walking barefoot on wet grass. He regretted that he had a job to do. But his regret did not spread to include Hall Avenue.

He entered 495 and walked to the directory. Theodore Boone was listed as being in Room 1804. Kling looked at his watch. It was 2:50. He nodded slightly and walked toward the elevator banks. He wore grey slacks and a grey-striped seersucker jacket. He did not at all look like a cop. With his blond hair and wide shoulders, with his long purposeful strides, he looked like a Scandinavian in America to study investment banking.

The elevator banks were divided into several sections. He

passed the Local 1-12 section, and then stopped at the Express 14-22 section, amused at the idea of a modern office building in the heart of a modern city superstitiously eliminating the thirteenth floor.

He stepped into the closest car and said, "Eighteen, please." The elevator operator stabbed a button.

"How's it outside?" the elevator operator asked.

"Nice."

"I never get out. I'm trapped in this building. From eight in the morning 'til five at night, I'm a prisoner. I never see the light. I have my lunch right here in the building. I bring my lunch, I eat it downstairs in a little room we got. I'm a mole."

Kling nodded sympathetically.

"This is a city of moles, you know that? I know people, they get off the subway, they walk underground to their office. At least I get the two-block walk to this building every morning and every night. Them, they get nothing. They walk underground to the office 'cause it's quicker, rain or shine. They eat their lunch in the arcade, underground. They go back to the subway underground when they leave the office at night. They never see the city. Me, I see two blocks of the city. How is it outside?"

"Nice," Kling said.

The starter snapped his fingers. The elevator operator closed the doors. "Eighteen, right?" he asked.

"Right," Kling said.

"Up and down all day long," the elevator operator said. "Up and down, but I'm never going any place. I'm a vertical mole. I'd rather be a subway conductor. Then at least I'd be a horizontal mole. And they come up for air. When they reach Calm's Point or Riverhead, the train comes up outa the ground. Me, up and down, up and down, all day long. It's nice outside, huh?"

"Very nice," Kling said.

"It seemed nice on the way to work this morning. You got an outside job, mister?"

"Part of the time," Kling said.

"Listen, even a part-time outside job is good," the elevator operator said. "I think I ought to get an outside job. Even maybe a street cleaner's job. That's outside."

"It gets cold in the winter," Kling said.

"Yeah?" This was a new idea to the elevator operator.

"Yeah, that's right, ain't it? Say, that's right." The car slid to a stop. "Eighteen," he said.

The door slid open. "Thank you," Kling said as he walked out of the car.

"Don't mention it," the elevator operator said. The door slid shut. Behind the door, the mechanism whirred and faded down the shaft. Kling smiled and looked for Room 1804. He followed the doors down the hallway and stopped before a set of double doors with frosted glass. He opened one of the doors and stepped into a small luxuriously furnished waiting room. A receptionist sat behind a desk at one end of the room. Kling walked directly to her.

"Mr. Boone," he said.

"Who shall I say is calling, please?"

"Detective Kling."

The girl looked up suddenly. "Are you a detective?"

"Yes," Kling said.

"Just a moment, sir."

She kept watching him as she pushed a toggle on her intercom.

"Yes?" a voice asked. Kling recognized it as Boone's.

"Detective Kling to see you, sir," the girl said, her eyes on Kling.

"Send him right in," Boone said. "I'm in the studio."

"Yes, sir." She flipped up her toggle and said, "Would you go in please, Mr. Kling? Through that door and then down the corridor. It's the last door."

"Thank you," Kling said. He opened the door, hesitated, and said, "Right or left?"

"What?"

"The corridor."

"Oh." The girl smiled. "Left down the corridor."

"Thank you," Kling said again. He closed the door behind him and turned left, walking past a series of doors. There was a door at the end of the corridor. He opened it and walked into a huge room which ran at a right angle to the corridor. A platform was set up at the far end of the room. A girl in a leopard skin was lying on a piece of black velvet which had been draped over the platform. Six lights were trained on the girl. A camera was trained on the girl. A man was behind the camera. Another man was arranging the folds in the velvet draped over the platform.

A third man stood with his arms folded, slightly to the left of the camera.

"I'd like to shoot up at her, Ted," the man with the folded arms said.

"I'll do whatever you want," Boone answered. "It's your ad."

"Well, that's what I'd like. I want to get the feeling she's looking down at us."

"What for?"

"It's what I want."

"But your copy reads 'Women look *up* to men who use Leopard Aftershave,' " Boone said.

"That's right," the man with the folded arms said.

"So why can't I look up?" the model in the leopard skin asked. "I photograph better looking up, anyway."

"I want you looking down."

"That doesn't make sense," the model said.

"Honey," the man with the folded arms said, "you're getting paid forty dollars an hour to pose, not to be an art director. When I want you to look up, I'll ask you to look up. Right now, I'd like you to look down, and I'd like our friend Mr. Boone to shoot from the floor to exaggerate this feeling of your looking down."

"Well, that's certainly a mystery to me," the girl said. "The copy says 'look up' and you want look down. That's certainly the mystery of the decade. That's certainly the inscrutable mystery of the Orient."

Kling cleared his throat.

Boone turned from the camera.

He was not a good-looking man, and yet he was a good-looking man. He was a trifle short perhaps, with thick black hair, and with the irregular features of a boxer. But he was narrow-waisted and wide-shouldered, and he turned with an economy of movement that told Kling he was quick on his feet and probably as sharply trained as a Commando. He had bright brown eyes, and they focused instantly on Kling, and he moved away from the camera just as instantly and walked to Kling with his hand extended.

"Detective Kling?" he asked.

"Yes," Kling said. "I hope I'm not intruding."

"Not at all." Boone turned and said, "Karl, mind if we take a short break?"

"I'm only paying the jungle queen forty dollars an hour," the man with the folded arms said.

"I can use a break," the model said. "This looking down bit can get strenuous."

"Go ahead," Karl said, unfolding his arms. "Take a break. Practice looking down. Practice looking down and giving the feeling that you're looking up at the same time."

"For that, you've got to be double-jointed," the model said. "You should have hired a circus performer."

"Sometimes I get the feeling I *have*," Karl said.

Kling followed Boone to the side of the room. He took a package of cigarettes from his pocket and extended it to Kling.

"Smoke?"

"Thanks, no," Kling said.

Boone shook a cigarette free and lighted it. He blew out a stream of smoke, sighed, and said, "Who killed her?"

"We don't know," Kling said.

"How can I help?"

"By answering some questions, if you don't mind."

"Not at all." Boone sucked in on his cigarette. "Shoot," he said.

"You were married how long?"

Boone did not stop to calculate. Quickly, he said, "Five years, two months, and eleven days."

"You remember that closely?"

"It was the happiest time of my life," Boone said.

"It was?" Kling said. His face was expressionless. He was remembering all that Mrs. Travail had told him, but his face remained expressionless.

"Yes," Boone said.

"Why'd you get divorced?"

"She didn't want me any more."

"Let me get this straight," Kling said. "*She* asked for the divorce?"

"Yes."

"Why?"

"I don't know. I wish I did know. I thought everything was going along fine. Christ knows, I loved her."

"We'd better start from the beginning," Kling said.

"All right. Where do you want me to start?"

"Where'd you meet?"

"At the public library."

38

"When was this?"

"Eight years ago. 1949?"

"Good enough. Remember the month?"

"June."

"What were you doing at the library?"

"I was free-lancing at the time. I'd had a job possibility, some industrial stuff, but I couldn't find any samples to clinch the deal. I'd had some stuff in one of the photography magazines, and I went to the library to locate the back issue."

"Did you?"

"Yes. I also met Annie."

"How?"

"It was strange. I guess I'm a nervous type. I was drumming my fingers on the table. I'd taken the . . . what do you call it . . . reader's guide to magazines or something, because I couldn't remember the issue the stuff had been in, and I was thumbing through it at the table and drumming my fingers. I'm a nervous type. Lots of nervous energy. I always tap a foot or drum my fingers or something. You know?"

"Go ahead."

"She was sitting at the table reading. She asked me to please stop drumming my fingers. I guess we had sort of a little argument about it. I wasn't really angry. She was a damned attractive girl, and I started the argument just so I could get to apologize later on."

"Did you?"

"Yes. I apologized and asked her out to dinner. She accepted. That was the beginning."

"What kind of a girl was Annie?"

"Annie?" Boone's eyes went reflectively sad. "The most wonderful girl I've ever met in my life. Alive, Mr. Kling. Really alive. You meet a lot of redheads who only have the red hair, and that's their fire. The rest is just washed-out pale complexion and no life. Have you noticed that most redheads have very pale complexions? When they get in the sun, they turn red all over, like lobsters. Annie wasn't that way. She was alive. Her red hair only set the pace. She loved doing things. Swimming, skiing, riding, everything. We had a ball. We really did. She didn't burn in the sun. She turned bronze. She was beautiful. I loved that girl. I gave that girl everything I had. I loved her."

"What happened?"

"I don't know."

"You don't have any inkling?"

Boone shrugged helplessly. "Monica was born. Have you met my daughter?"

"Yes."

"She's a charmer, isn't she?"

"Yes."

"Then you've met the Bag, too?"

"What? I'm sorry."

"My ex mother-in-law. Mrs. Travail."

"Yes. I met her."

"The bitch," Boone said. "I'm taking her to court, you know."

"I didn't know."

"For custody of the child."

"I got the impression she liked you," Kling said.

"Really? She's a great actress, the Bag. I think she had more to do with Annie and me splitting up than anything else."

"How do you figure that?"

"She hated Annie. The Bag lost all her men, and she didn't like the idea that her daughter had one. The Bag also lost her looks, and Annie still had hers. The Bag was stupid, Annie was bright."

"Bright?"

"Intelligent. Smart as a whip. There wasn't anything Annie couldn't do and do well. A quick learner, Mr. Kling. Quick. I had a hard time keeping up with her."

"She . . . she wasn't stupid?"

"Stupid? Hell, no. She was that rare combination, a brain with good looks. And she didn't flaunt the brain. She didn't make you feel like an idiot. Oh, Jesus, Mr. Kling, how can I tell you about Annie? She was the best thing that ever happened to me. She's responsible for whatever I am now. I was a dumb kid with a camera when I met her. Now I know what I want out of life, now I know the things that are important. Annie did all that. The day I lost her was the blackest day of my life."

"You were trying to explain why you got divorced."

"Oh. Yeah. Well, Monica was born. You can't have so much fun when you've got an infant on your hands. I mean, no matter how much you love the child, you're still

40

tied down. Annie wouldn't leave her with anyone but the Bag. She wanted the Bag to come live with us. I flatly refused. I didn't see why we couldn't get baby sitters, the way other young married people do. Annie wouldn't. She simply wouldn't. She loved that kid like . . . well, she loved her. But at the same time, I think she resented her. Because she tied us down, do you know? Because we couldn't go off on those long ski weekends anymore. Because we couldn't pack up and go to the beach for a week on a moment's notice."

"What else?" Kling asked.

"Well, I hate to admit this . . ."

"Yes."

"She was outgrowing me."

"What?"

"I'm a camera. That's really all I am. Photography is my profession, and I see everything as if I'm looking through a camera. I feel things that way, Mr. Kling. I'm one of those people who . . . who feel things. But I'm not much in the brain department, never was."

"I see," Kling said.

"Annie was growing. I wasn't. Cameras don't grow, Mr. Kling, they only record."

"Annie outgrew *you?*"

"Yes."

"Not the other way around?"

"Oh, don't be ridiculous. God, she had a mind like a trap. Click! A hungry mind. Devoured things. Wonderful. A wonderful girl."

"Why'd she go to work in a liquor store after she divorced you?"

"I don't know. A girl like her, I figured she'd want a challenge. Advertising, radio, television, something like that, something where she could use her mind. So first she works selling furniture, and then liquor. I didn't get it. I asked her once. When I went up to see Monica."

"What did she say?"

"She said, 'I need a rest, Ted. Everybody has to rest every now and then.' Well, she got her rest."

"I should imagine, if what you said was accurate, that she'd had enough of a rest. Being cooped up with the child, I mean."

"Yes," Boone said. "That's what I would have thought."

He dropped his cigarette to the floor and stepped on it.

"Then why'd she take those jobs?"

"I don't know."

"Did you argue much, Mr. Boone? When you were married to her?"

"The usual. You know how marriage is."

"Once a week? Twice a week?"

"Oh, I don't know. I never kept count. You know how marriage is. Two people get on each other's nerves every now and then. So an argument starts. I never kept count."

"Would you say you were happily married?"

Boone hesitated. At last he said, "No."

"Why not?"

"I guess . . . I guess I wasn't enough for Annie."

"Were there any other men in her life?"

"No. You don't think they'd have given her custody of the child if there were, do you?"

"And you? Another woman?"

"No. Annie was enough for me."

"But you weren't enough for her?"

"No."

"And yet, there were no other men?"

"No. None that I know of. Adultery was never an issue. We couldn't have got a divorce in this state if we'd wanted to."

"Did you want custody of the child?"

"No. Not at the time of the divorce. I didn't want anything to remind me of Annie."

"Because you loved her so much?"

"Yes. After a while, I realized I was behaving stupidly. I sought her out. Her and Monica. I went to see them. My daughter loves me, Mr. Kling. I've got a good relationship with my daughter. I want her to live with me. I can give her things the Bag can never give her. The Bag's holding her illegally. The courts awarded that child to Annie, not to my mother-in-law. She's holding her illegally, and if the god-damn courts weren't so slow, I'd have Monica *now*."

"You said you didn't want Monica at first, is that right?"

"Yes."

"And you loved Annie very much?"

"Very much."

"Tell me, Mr. Boone. When you were divorced, did you

ever think there was any chance of you and Annie getting together again?"

"In the beginning, I did."

"For how long?"

"Six months or so. I kept thinking she'd call me. Especially when I found out she'd got a job selling furniture. I kept thinking she'd call me and try to patch it up. For about six months, I kept hoping that."

"She didn't call."

"No."

"And during this time, you made no attempt to see either her or Monica, is that right?"

"That's right."

"When did you see Monica again? After the divorce, I mean."

"About six or seven months after the divorce."

"Did you ever ask Annie for custody of the child?"

"Well . . . yes."

"And?"

"She refused. She felt the child's place was with her mother."

"I see. Did you ever try to do anything about it legally?"

"I consulted a lawyer. He said the courts had awarded the child to Annie, and that was it."

"There was no chance, then, of your gaining legal possession of the child."

"Well, there is now. The Bag has no claim to her. After all, she's *my* daughter."

"Yes, now there's a possibility. I didn't mean that, Mr. Boone. I meant, while Annie was alive."

"Oh. No, no. While Annie was alive, I couldn't have the child. I could visit her, of course, and she could spend time with me. I had her for a month every now and then. But I couldn't have her with me all the time. No. Not while Annie was alive. Things are different now. I'll fight the Bag if it takes every cent I've got."

Kling sighed. "When was the last time you saw Annie, Mr. Boone?"

"About three weeks ago."

"What was the occasion?"

"I went to see Monica. Annie happened to be home. Usually, I tried to time my visits so that I wouldn't run into her."

"Were you friendly on that occasion?"

"We were always friendly."

"No arguments?"

"None."

"Did custody of the child come up?"

"No. That was a closed issue as far as I was concerned. I knew I couldn't have her, and so I made the best of it. Now, things are different. The moment Annie died, I looked into it. The Bag doesn't stand a chance. That's why I've started the legal machinery going."

"*When* did you start, Mr. Boone?"

"When Annie died."

"The same day?"

"The day after."

"Do you own a gun, Mr. Boone?"

"Yes."

"What make and calibre?"

"It's an Iver Johnson. A .22."

"Do you have a pistol permit?"

"Yes."

"Carry or premises?"

"Premises. It's just a small gun, you know. I keep it for protection at home. I live on the South Side in Stewart City. That's an expensive part of Isola. A lot of burglaries there. I keep the gun for protection."

"Do you have any other pistols?"

"No."

"A .25 perhaps?"

"No."

"Just that one gun? A .22 Iver Johnson, right?"

"Yes."

"Did Annie have any enemies that you know of?"

"No. She was well-liked by everyone."

"What's your lawyer's name?"

"My lawyer?"

"Yes."

"Why do you want to know his name?"

"I'd like to talk to him."

"About what?"

"Routine," Kling said.

Boone studied him for a moment. "Jefferson Dobberly," he said at last.

"Do you know where I can reach him?"

"His offices are downtown in the Meredith Street section. 413 Margaret Place. Do you want his number?"

"If you have it handy."

"Cooke 4-8310," Boone said.

Kling wrote it into his pad. "Thank you, Mr. Boone," he said. "I hope you'll be available if any further questions come to mind." He took a card from his wallet. "If you should happen to remember anything you feel is important, just call me, won't you. The 87th Squad, Detective Kling. The number's on the card."

Boone took the card and studied it.

From the other side of the room, Karl—standing with his arms folded—said, "Hey, Ted, can we get this show on the road? The jungle queen's getting rich."

"I've got to get back to work," Boone said.

"I appreciate the time you've given me," Kling said.

"One thing, Mr. Kling."

"Yes?"

"You don't think I did this, do you?"

"You know the answer to that one, Mr. Boone," Kling said.

"Come on, Ted," Karl called. "Let's go."

"Okay, okay," Boone said. "Good luck, Mr. Kling." And then he turned his back and walked toward the model and said, "Now let's get this jazz right this time, okay?"

CHAPTER 6

IT WAS funny the way Detective Roger Havilland got killed.

Now there are certainly a good many people who don't think there is anything funny whatever about getting killed, no matter how you happen to get killed. And the way Roger Havilland got killed wasn't really a funny ha-ha way, it was simply funny-peculiar. But it was funny. No question about it. If you knew Roger Havilland at all, you had to admit it was funny.

It wasn't easy to be Havilland.

He was a big man if you consider six feet four inches and two hundred and twenty pounds big. Maybe you don't. There are a lot of men who consider that average, and a lot of women who like their men to look like Primo Carnera. Maybe you're one of them. Maybe you think Havilland was a midget.

The cops at the 87th thought he was pretty big, but that's because they had seen Havilland in action. He was not easy to miss when he was in action. He used his hands a lot. He liked to *hit* people, so to speak. Well, maybe he didn't really like to hit them, but he *did* hit them all the time, and it seemed as if he enjoyed it while he was doing it.

Cops like Steve Carella and Bert Kling didn't find it strange that Havilland enjoyed hitting people. They knew why he did. They didn't approve of it, but they knew why. They disliked him intensely. There wasn't a cop in the 87th, uniformed or detective, who really liked Havilland. They were sorry he got it, but not because they really liked him. They just didn't like to see cops getting killed. It made them think about becoming plumbers or bartenders.

Havilland, however, had once been a nice cop. That's the truth. Carella knew him when, and Meyer knew him when, and Lieutenant Byrnes knew him when, and a lot of other cops at the 87th knew Havilland before he became a bull.

He became a Havilland-bull as differentiated from a Carella-bull or a Kling-bull. He became a *real* bull. A bull who snorted and farted and burped and gored and roared and boffed like a bull. A bull. Havilland was simply a bull.

He became a bull because he decided there was no percentage in being a nice-type happy-guy smiling-faced cop. The way he decided was like this.

He was walking along one day minding his own business when he spotted a street fight in progress, and it seemed as if a lot of kids were ganging up on one nice-type happy-guy smiling-faced kid, and so Havilland stepped in like a hero. The kids, who'd been content up to then to be bashing in the head of a fellow street fighter, decided it would be more fun to play the *Anvil Chorus* on the head of Roger Havilland. Havilland had drawn his service revolver by that time, and he very politely fired a few shots into the air to let the boys know the Law was on the scene. One of the boys, not being terribly impressed by the Law, brought a lead pipe down on Havilland's right wrist and knocked the gun from his hand. That was when the other boys became musicians in earnest.

They played a chorus of *Chopsticks* and then a few bars of *Night on Bald Mountain* and then they did their famous version of *To a Wild Rose,* by which time they had succeeded in breaking Havilland's arm in four places. They also succeeded in leaving his face looking like a pound of chopped chuck, ground twice, thank you.

The compound fracture hurt. It hurt like hell. It hurt worse than hell because the doctors had to break the arm all over again since it would not set properly the first time around. Havilland had just made Detective 3rd/Grade, and he thought perhaps the broken arm would kick him clear off the force. It didn't. It healed. Roger Havilland was a whole man again, except for the queer mental quirk his do-gooder intrusion had produced. He had, of course, been on the business end of a lead pipe before. No cop in the 87th survived very long if he didn't know how to cope with an arm swinging a lead pipe or a ball bat or a wrench or a broom or any one of a number of homemade weapons. But he had never been beat up while actually trying to help someone. Havilland even suspected that the kid he'd been trying to help was one of those who'd kicked him after he'd fallen and was dragged into an alley. This was certainly no way to treat a good Samaritan. This wasn't even a way to treat a bad Samaritan.

Sitting alone in his hospital room, Havilland figured it out. As far as he was concerned, they could all go and. Every last one of them could go and. Their mothers could go and. Their fathers could go and. The whole world could go and. Roger Havilland was watching out for Number One. Everybody else could go and. In Macy's window.

It was unfortunate.

A lot of people suffered because of what half a dozen kids did to Roger Havilland a long time ago.

Looking at it in another way, if Havilland had had the gumption to stick to his original premise, he might still be alive today. That's the trouble with people. You find a streak of human nature in almost every one of them. If Havilland could have stuck to being an out-and-out rat, he'd have been all right. No. He had to get noble.

Which is why it was funny the way he got killed.

He had left the squad at about 10:35. He'd told Carella and Hawes, who were working with him, that he wanted to check the streets. Actually, he was going down to get a cup of coffee, and then he would go home. When he got home, he would call Carella and say, "Everything's quiet. I'm heading home." When a cop's been on the force awhile, he learns these little tricks.

It was a pretty nice night and Havilland, only because he wanted a little air before he went into the subway, decided he really would walk around the streets a little. He was not looking for trouble. Havilland was one of those cops who consciously avoid trouble. If trouble came to Havilland, he would not back away from it. But look for it? No. Not Havilland. He would leave that to the heroes. The world was full of heroes.

Sometimes, the streets of the 87th were nice. It didn't have anything to do with the people in them. Havilland hated the people in the streets of the 87th. As far as he was concerned, all spics could go and. All kikes could go and.

All wops could go and. All niggers could go and. In fact, all *people* could go and. Except Number One.

It was just that sometimes everything got quiet in the streets and you could feel the heartbeat of a city there, especially on a night close to summer when the sky was a shade of off-black, and the moon hung in the sky like a whore's belly button, and you could smell the perfume of the city. On nights like that, Havilland remembered perhaps that he'd been born in the city, and that he'd once played Kick the Can on the city's streets, and that he'd once been in love with an Irish girl named Peggy Muldoon. This was a night like that.

So he walked the streets of the precinct, and he didn't say hello to anybody because everybody could go and. But he walked with his shoulders back and his head high and a sort of lopsided grin on his massive face, and he felt pretty good, even though he hated to admit it to himself.

There was a grocery store at the end of the street, and the man who owned the grocery store was called Tony Rigatoni, and everybody called him Tony-Tony, and Havilland decided he would stop in on Tony-Tony to say hello, even though he didn't particularly like Tony-Tony. It didn't hurt a man to say hello to someone before he went into the subway.

That is when the funny thing happened.

As Havilland approached Tony-Tony's grocery, he saw that someone was sitting on the sidewalk in front of the store. The person was well dressed and didn't look at all like a hood or a wino, and perhaps Havilland had drunk too deeply of the heady June air. Whatever the reason, Havilland didn't walk up to the man and say, "Get on your feet, punk," as was his wont to do. He sort of ambled over to him slowly and casually and then, standing in front of the plate glass window of the shop, he politely inquired, "Are you all right, mister?"

Now this was a throwback to the day Havilland had stepped into that street brawl to defend the kid who was getting his lumps. This was a definite throwback, and perhaps Havilland felt that warning trigger click someplace inside his head because his hand snapped slightly upwards toward his shoulder holster, but it snapped too late.

The man on the sidewalk got up with a sudden lurch.

He threw his shoulder against Havilland's chest and sent him flying backwards into the plate glass window. Then he ran off down the sidewalk.

Havilland didn't know that Tony-Tony was lying behind the counter of his grocery, badly beaten. He did not know that the young man had entered Tony-Tony's store and held him up, or that Tony-Tony had fired a shot from the .22 he kept under the cash register as the young man was departing. He did not know that Tony-Tony had collapsed from his beating immediately afterwards, or that the young man on the sidewalk was carrying a .22 calibre slug in his shoulder, which had dumped him on the sidewalk in the first place. He didn't know any of these things.

Havilland knew only that he was flying backwards, off balance. He knew only that he collided with the plate glass window, and that the window shattered around him in a thousand flying fragments of sharp splinters. He felt sudden pain, and he yelled, with something close to tears in his voice, "You bastard! You dirty bastard! You can go and . . ." but that was all he said. He never said another word.

One of the shards of glass had pierced his jugular vein and another had pierced his windpipe, and that was the end of Roger Havilland.

Around the corner, the young man got into a 1947 Dodge and drove away. An old lady saw him screech away from the curb. She did not notice the license plate number of the car. When the car had left, she bent down to examine the sidewalk and blinked when her hands came away wet with blood.

There were a lot of old ladies around the grocery store when Detective Cotton Hawes arrived. He had left Carella back at the squad and hopped into a patrol car the moment the squeal came in. He stepped out of the car now, and the crowd parted respectfully because this was the Law, and Cotton Hawes indeed looked like the Law. His red head towered above the crowd, the white streak looking like the lightning crease on the head of Captain Ahab. Or at least on the head of Gregory Peck.

The patrolman standing in the grocery store doorway walked to him as he approached. He did not recognize Hawes. He blinked at him.

"I'm Detective Hawes," Hawes said. "Steve Carella's catching. He sent me out."

"This ain't so good," the patrolman said.

"What isn't?"

"Proprietor of the store's been beat up bad. Cash register's been cleaned out. You know Havilland?"

"Havilland who?"

"Rog Havilland. He's on the squad."

"I was introduced to him," Hawes said, nodding. "What about him?"

"He's sitting in the window."

"What?"

"He's dead." The patrolman grinned slightly. "Funny, huh? Who'd have ever thought anything could kill Rog Havilland?"

"I don't see anything funny about it," Hawes said. "Get this crowd back. Is the proprietor inside?"

"Yes, sir," the patrolman said.

"I'm going in. Get into the crowd and get the names and addresses of any eyewitnesses. Do you know how to write?"

"Huh? Of course I know how to write."

"Then start writing," Hawes said, and he went into the shop.

Tony Rigatoni was sitting in a chair, a second patrolman standing alongside him. Hawes spoke to the patrolman first.

"Call Carella," he said. "Tell him we've got a homicide. This was reported as a stickup. Tell him the corpse is Roger Havilland. Do it quick."

"Yes, sir," the patrolman said, and he left the shop.

"I'm Detective Hawes," Hawes said to Rigatoni. "I don't think I know your name, sir."

"Rigatoni."

"What happened, Mr. Rigatoni?"

He looked at Rigatoni's face. Whoever had beaten him had done a merciless job.

"This man come in the shop," Rigatoni said. "He tell me empty the cash register. I tell him go to hell. He hit me."

"What'd he use?"

"His hands. He wear gloves. In June. He hit me hard. He keep hitting me. The shade on my door, he pulled down when he come in, you know?"

"Go ahead."

"He come around behind the counter and empty the register. I got the whole day receipts in there."

"How much?"

"Two hundred, three hundred, something like. Son of a bitch takes it."

"Where were you?"

"On the floor. He beat me bad. I could hardly stand. He starts running out the shop. I get up. I keep a gun in the drawer under the register. A .22. I got a license, don't worry. I shoot him."

"Did you hit him?"

"I think so. I think I see him fall. Then I get dizzy, and I collapse."

"How'd Havilland crash that window?"

"Who the hell is Havilland?"

"The detective who smashed through your window."

"I didn't know he was a bull. I don't know how that happened. I was out."

"When'd you come to?"

"Five minutes ago. Just before I called the cops."

"How old was this man? The one who held you up?"

"Twenty-three, twenty-four. No older."

"White or colored?"

"White."

"What color hair?"

"Blond."

"Eyes?"

"I don't know."

"Didn't you notice?"

"No."

"How was he dressed?"

"A sports jacket. A sports shirt, no tie. Gloves. Black gloves."

"Did he have a gun?"

"If he had one, he didn't use it."

"Mustache?"

"No. He was a kid."

"Notice any scars, birthmarks, anything like that?"

"No."

"Was he alone?"

"All alone."

"Did he walk away or drive away?"

"I don't know. I told you. I was out. Like a light. Son of a bitch almost broke my jaw. I ever see him again . . ."

"Excuse me, sir," one of the patrolmen said from the door.

Hawes turned. "What is it?"

"We got an old lady out here."

"Yeah?"

"Says she saw the guy get into a car and drive away."

"I'll talk to her," Hawes said, and he walked out of the shop.

"This is her," the patrolman said.

Hawes looked at the woman. It would have been easy to believe, at first glance, that the woman was a crackpot. She had straggly grey hair which she had not bothered to comb since she had grown it. In all likelihood, she had not washed since the city had had its last water-scarcity scare. She wore a tattered green shawl and shoes which looked as if they belonged to her grandson who was stationed with the Air Force in Alaska. A faded red rose was pinned to the green shawl. And to substantiate the early impression of a crackpot, one of the other women in the crowd whispered, "That's Crazy Connie."

It would have been easy to believe she was a crackpot.

But even in a precinct like the 30th, Hawes had learned that the ones who look like crackpots are very often sane and reliable witnesses. In fact, the sober-looking citizens very often turned out to be the nuts. So he gently led the old woman away from the crowd and into the grocery store, holding her elbow, the way he would have held the elbow of his own grandmother. Crazy Connie seemed to enjoy the notoriety. She looked up at Hawes as if she had won him on a blind date and was terribly pleased with her good fortune. Hawes, grinning like a courtier, led her to a chair.

"Won't you sit down, madam?" he said.

"Miss," Crazy Connie corrected.

"Ah yes, of course. What is your name, Miss?"

"Connie," she answered. "Connie Fitzhenry." Her voice was clear and bold. It did not at all sound like the voice of a crackpot.

"Miss Fitzhenry," Hawes said pleasantly, "one of the patrolmen tells me you saw a man get into a car and drive away. Is that right?"

"What's *your* name?" Connie asked.

"Detective Hawes," he said.

"How do you do?"

"How do you do? Is that right?"

"Is *what* right, sir?" Connie asked.

"That you saw a man get into a car and drive away?"

"I did indeed," Connie said. "Do you know how old I am?"

"How old, Miss Fitzhenry?"

"Seventy-four. Do I look seventy-four?"

"I would say you weren't a day, over sixty."

"Would you really?"

"I would really."

"Thank you."

"About this man . . ."

"He came running around the corner," Connie said, "and he got into a car and drove away. I saw him."

"Was he carrying a gun?"

"No, sir."

"Any other weapon?"

"No, sir."

"What makes you think he was the man who held up Mr. Rigatoni?"

"I didn't say I thought he was the man who held up anyone. I'm only saying he came around the corner and got into a car and drove away."

"I see," Hawes said, and he began to think he'd judged wrongly this time. Connie Fitzhenry was showing all the signs of a first-grade crackpot. "What I'm driving at, Miss Fitzhenry," he said, "is why you felt the man was in any way suspicious."

"I got my reasons," Connie said.

"What are they?"

"My reasons."

"Yes, but . . ."

"You think this young man held up Mr. Rigatoni?" Connie asked.

"Well, we're trying to . . ."

"What did he look like?" Connie asked.

"Well . . ."

"What color hair did he have?"

"Blond," Hawes said.

"Mmm-huh. Eyes?"

"We don't know."

"What was he wearing?"

"A sports shirt with no tie. A sports jacket. And black gloves," Hawes answered, suddenly wondering how he had got on the wrong end of the interrogation stick. He looked at Connie. Connie wasn't saying a word. "Well?" he asked.

"Well what?"

"Well, is that the man you saw?"

"That's the man I saw, all right."

"Well!" Hawes said. "Now we're getting somewhere."

"I knew there was something fishy as soon as he pulled away from the curb," Connie said. "I didn't need your description."

"What made you think so?"

"Why, the man was bleeding," Connie said. "His blood is all over the sidewalk around the corner."

Hawes nodded to the patrolman, and the patrolman left the shop to check on Connie's statement.

"Did you happen to notice the license plate on the car?"

"Yes, I noticed it," Connie said.

"What number was it?"

"Oh, I didn't notice the number. I just noticed there was a license plate on the car."

"What year and make was the car?" Hawes asked. "Would you know that?"

"Of course I would. You don't think I do, do you? You don't think a seventy-four-year-old woman wonders about such things. Well, I can tell you the year and make of any car on the road. I've got good eyes. Twenty-twenty vision even though I'm seventy-four years old."

"What was the . . ."

"That car across the street there is a 1954 Buick. The one behind it is a Ford station wagon, 1952. The one . . ."

"How about the one that man got into?" Hawes asked.

"You don't think I know, do you?"

"I think you do know," Hawes said. "I just wish you'd tell me."

Connie grinned crookedly. "It was a 1947 Dodge."

"Sedan?"

"Yes."

"Four-door or two?"

"Four-door."

"What color?"

"Green. Not the manufacturer's green. The Chrysler Corporation never put a coat of green like that on any of their cars."

"What sort of green was it?"

"Almost a Kelly green. That car'd been repainted. That wasn't the original paint job."

"Are you sure?"

"I can tell you any car on the road. I'm good on cars. I never saw an original paint job like that one. Not even today with the crazy colors they're putting on cars."

"Well, thanks a lot, Miss Fitzhenry," Hawes said. "You've certainly been a help." He was leading her to the doorway of the grocery store. She stopped, smiled up at him pleasantly, her crooked teeth showing.

"Don't you want my address?" she asked.

"What for, Miss Fitzhenry?"

"So you'll know where to send the check," she said.

CHAPTER 7

IN THE squad room, Bert Kling was talking on the phone to his fiancée, Claire Townsend.

"I can't talk," he said.

"Can't you even say you love me?"

"No," he said.

"Why not?"

"Because."

"Is someone standing near your desk?"

"Yes."

"Who?"

"Meyer."

"Did you call me?" Meyer asked, turning.

"No. No, Meyer."

"*Do* you love me?" Claire asked.

"Yes," Kling said. He glanced surreptitiously at Meyer. Meyer was not a fool, and he probably knew exactly what Claire was asking, and was probably enjoying Kling's discomfort immensely. Kling would never understand women. A beautiful girl like Claire, a sensible girl like Claire, should realize that a Detective Squad Room was not the place to be bandying about words of love and devotion. He formed a mental picture of her as she spoke, the black void of her hair, the brown depths of her eyes, the narrow nose, the high cheek bones, the curved length of her body.

"Tell me you love me," she said.

"What are you doing?" he asked.

"I'm studying."

"For what?"

"A sociology exam."

"Good. Go study. If you want to graduate this semester . . ."

"Will you marry me when I graduate?"

"Not until you get a job."

"If you were a lieutenant, I wouldn't have to get a job."

"I know, but I'm only a Detective/3rd."

"This is my last exam."

"Did you pass the others?"

"Snaps."

"Good. Go study."

"I'd rather talk to you."

"I'm busy. You're wasting the taxpayers' time."

"All right, Conscientious."

"Conscientious, anyone?" Kling asked, and Claire burst out laughing.

"That does it," she said. "Goodbye. Will you call me tonight?"

"Yes."

"I love you, cop," she said, and she hung up.

"The girl friend?" Meyer asked.

"Mmm," Kling said.

"*L'amour,* it's wonderful," Meyer said.

"Go to hell."

"I'm serious. June, moon, spoon, croon. When's the wedding?"

"Not *this* June, that's for sure."

"Next June?"

"Maybe sooner."

"Good," Meyer said. "Get married. There's nothing like marriage for a cop. It gives him a sense of justice. He knows already what it feels like to be a prisoner, so he doesn't hurry to make false arrests."

"Baloney," Kling said. "You love it."

"Who said no?" Meyer asked. "Been married to the same woman for almost thirteen years now, God bless her." His blue eyes twinkled. "I'm getting used to my cell. I think if she left the door unlocked, I wouldn't even try to escape."

"You've got it real tough," Kling said.

"I love her," Meyer said philosophically. "What can I do? I'm a sucker for this love bit. Sue me."

"Were you a cop when you married her?"

"Sure. We met in college. That was in . . ."

"I didn't know you went to college."

"I'm a big intellectual," Meyer said. "You mean you

didn't know? Can't you tell looking at me? I come from a long line of scholars. In the town in Europe where my grandfather came from, he was the only man who could read and write. An honor. A great honor."

"I believe it," Kling said.

"You should. Have you ever known me to tell a falsehood? Never. Honest John Meyer, they call me. I studied law in college, did you know that?"

"No," Kling said.

"Sure. But when I got out of school, people needed lawyers like they needed holes in the head. I got out of school in 1940. You know what people needed then? Not lawyers."

"What?"

"Soldiers."

"Oh."

"Yeah. Uncle Sam wagged his finger. I went. I had a choice? When I got out in 1944, I didn't feel like being a lawyer anymore. All of a sudden, I didn't feel like struggling in a little cubbyhole office, chasing ambulances. I joined the force. That's when I married Sarah."

"Mazeltov," Kling said, smiling.

"Gesundheit," Meyer replied, and the telephone rang. Meyer picked it up. "Detective Meyer, 87th Squad," he said. "Who? Yes, he's here. Who's this, please? Okay, just a second." He covered the mouthpiece. "A guy named Ted Boone," he said to Kling. "Any relation to the dead girl?"

"Her ex-husband," Kling said. "I'll take it." Meyer handed him the phone. "Hello?" Kling said.

"Detective Kling? This is Ted Boone."

"Yes, how are you, Mr. Boone?"

"Fine, thank you."

"What is it?"

"Something that might interest you. I don't know. I just went down to the mailbox. There was a letter in it. From Annie."

"Annie?"

"Yes. It was wrongly addressed, mailed last week some time. I guess the wrong address explains why it took so long to get here. Anyway, it was rather weird."

"Yes. Anything important in it?"

"Well, I'll let you judge for yourself. Can you come over?"

"Are you still home?"

"Yes."

"What's the address?" Kling asked. Boone gave it to him. "I'll be right over," Kling said, and he hung up.

"Anything?" Meyer asked.

"Might be."

"Not sure?"

"No."

"Why don't you ask Detective Cotton Hawes?" Meyer said, his eyes twinkling again. "I hear he's a regular whiz."

"And good day to you," Kling said, and then shoved his way through the slatted rail divider and walked out of the squad room.

Stewart City had been named after British royalty. It was a compact little area of Isola, running for perhaps three square blocks midtown, three square blocks that hugged the curve of the River Dix. Stewart City had been named after British royalty, and the apartment buildings which faced the river in terraced luxury were indeed royal. There was a time when the North Side of Isola had claimed the fashionable addresses, but those addresses had slowly become dowdy so that a River Harb apartment was no longer considered *haut monde*. Many River Harb apartments, in fact, were part of the 87th Precinct, and the 87th Precinct could hardly be called a fashionable part of the city.

Stewart City *was* fashionable. The *entire* South Side was not fashionable, but Stewart City was. You could not get very much more fashionable than Stewart City was fashionable.

Bert Kling felt somewhat like the country mouse visiting the city mouse. His clothes felt suddenly out of style. His walk seemed loutish. He wondered if the hayseed of the slums was showing in his blond hair.

The doorman at Stewart Terrace looked at him as if he were a grocery boy who'd come to the front door when he should have been making deliveries in the rear. Nonetheless, he held the door open for Kling and Kling entered a foyer done in the coolest modern he had ever seen. He felt as if he had stepped into a Picasso painting by accident. He felt he would be dripped on by a Dali watch at any moment. He felt trapped in the prison of a Mondrian.

Hastily, he walked to the directory, found Boone's name, and then walked to the elevator bank. He buzzed and waited.

When the elevator arrived, the operator asked. "Whom did you wish to see, sir?"

"Ted Boone," he answered.

"Sixth floor," the operator said.

"I know," Kling said.

"I see." The doors slid shut. The elevator moved into action. The operator studied Kling disdainfully. "Are you a model?" he asked.

"No."

"I didn't think so," the operator said, as if this was one point for his side.

"Does Mr. Boone have many models coming to his apartment?"

"Not *male* models," the operator said disdainfully. "You're a cop, aren't you?"

"Yes."

"I can always tell a cop," the operator said. "They have a distinct aroma about them."

"I'm demolished," Kling said. "You pierced my disguise."

"Ha," the operator said.

"I'm really an old old man with a beard. I didn't think you'd tip so easily. It must be that distinct aroma."

"You here about Boone's ex-wife?" the operator asked, smugly knowledgeable.

"Are *you* a detective?" Kling said.

"Come on," the operator said, slightly insulted.

"I thought you might be. You interrogate excellently. Come over to the precinct. We may have a spot for you."

"Ha, ha," the operator said.

"I'm serious." Kling paused. "But you're not five eight, are you?"

The operator stood erect. "I'm five *eleven*."

"Oh, good. Over twenty-one?"

"I'm twenty-*four!*"

"Excellent, excellent! 20/20 vision without glasses?"

"Perfect eyesight."

"Have a criminal record?"

"Certainly not!" the operator said indignantly.

"Then you've got a career ahead of you with the police

department," Kling said. "And you can start at the fabulous salary of close to $3800 a year, which is probably half what you make in this place. But think of the advantages. You can stand around and take all kinds of snide remarks from the public if you're a cop. It's wonderful. Nothing like it. Makes a man out of you."

"I'm not interested."

"What's the matter?" Kling asked. "Don't you want to be a man?"

"Six," the operator said, and he looked at Kling disdainfully when he let him out of the car, and then slammed the door behind him.

Kling walked down the corridor, found Boone's door, and pushed the buzzer set in the jamb. From within the house, Kling heard a series of chimes playing a tune. He didn't recognize the tune at first because it was more intricate than anything he had ever heard on a set of chimes before. He pushed the buzzer again.

"The photographers will snap us," the chimes chimed, *"and you'll find that you're in the rotogravure."*

Irving Berlin, Kling thought. *Easter Parade.* Photographers must be making good money these days if they can afford chimes that play parts of *Easter Parade.* I wonder if Boone would like to be a cop. Good starting salary, opportunity for advancement, excellent working con . . .

The door opened.

Boone was standing in it. He wore a Chinese robe which was seven sizes too large for him. "Come in," he said. "I was dressing. I've got a sitting in a half hour."

Kling stepped into the apartment and then understood the Chinese robe. Apparently, Boone was fascinated with things Oriental. The room was furnished in what seemed to be authentic Chinese. There were rare old pieces of teak furniture, and heavy pieces of jade sculpture. The drapes on the window were a Chinese print. A rice-paper screen was opened behind an old Chinese writing desk. Chinese pictures were on the wall. Kling fully expected the smell of chow mein from the kitchen.

Noticing his scrutiny, Boone said, "I was stationed in China during the war. Ever there?"

"No," Kling said.

"Fell in love with the place. The most wonderful people in the world. You ought to go sometime."

"It's a little different now, I imagine," Kling said.

"The Reds, you mean? Terrible. But that'll pass. Everything changes sooner or later. Do you want to see that letter?"

"That's why I came."

"I'll get it. You don't mind if I dress while you read it, do you? I've got to get to the studio."

"Not at all," Kling said.

"Sit down. Make yourself comfortable. Like a drink?"

"No, thank you."

"Cigarettes there on the coffee table. That brass cigarette box is from Hong Kong," Boone said as he left the room.

"Thanks," Kling said. He sat, lifted the lid from the box, took out a cigarette and lighted it. The cigarette tasted peculiar. Either it was very stale, or it too had come from Hong Kong. He squashed it out and lighted one of his own. In a few moments, Boone came back. He had taken off the robe and was wearing trousers and a white shirt, the white shirt hanging out of the trousers, unbuttoned.

"Here's the letter," he said. "You read it. I'll be back in a few minutes." Buttoning the shirt, he left the room again.

The envelope was a pale blue rectangle. Annie Boone had addressed it in deep blue ink. She had addressed it to "Mr. Ted Boone" at 585 Tarlton Place. The middle digit in the address was wrong. If Annie had ever known the correct address, she had apparently forgotten it. The Post Office Department had penciled its scrawls across the face of the envelope. The last scrawl advised, "Try 565 Tarlton." Apparently, 565 had been tried and the letter had finally been delivered.

Kling lifted the flap and pulled out the letter.

Annie Boone wrote in a small clear hand. The letter was neat and unstained and showed no signs of having been written hurriedly. It was dated Friday, June 7th, three days before she'd been murdered. Today was June 14th. Annie Boone had been dead four days. Roger Havilland had been killed last night. The letter read:

> *Ted dear:*
> *I know how you feel about Monica, and I know what you're trying to do, and I suppose I should harbor ill will, but something has come up and I*

63

would like very much to talk to you about it. You are, after all, perhaps the one person I could always talk to.

I received a letter yesterday, Ted, and it's frightened me, and I want to know whether or not I should go to the police. I tried to reach you by telephone both at home and at the studio, but they told me you were away in Connecticut and would not be back until Monday. This will be waiting for you when you return, and I hope you'll call me at once, either at home or at the liquor store. The number at the store is CAmbridge 7-6200. Please call.

My best,
Annie

Kling read the letter once, and then read it again. He was reading it a third time when Boone came back into the room. Boone had put on a tie and a sports jacket, and he seemed distinctly all-American in the all-Chinese room.

"Have you tried these cigarettes?" Boone asked, taking one from the brass box. "They're British."

"I tried them," Kling said. "About this letter, Mr. Boone."

Boone lighted the cigarette and then glanced at his watch. "I have a few minutes yet," he said. "What do you make of it?"

"May I ask you a few questions?"

"Certainly."

"First, why *'Ted dear'* instead of the usual salutation? This implies more affection than I was led to believe existed."

"Not affection," Boone said. "Affectation. She used that reverse salutation with everyone, believe me." He shrugged. "Just a part of Annie, that's all. Means nothing."

"What does this mean?" Kling asked. " *'I know how you feel about Monica, and I know what you're trying to do . . .'* "

"Oh. Nothing."

"Well, explain what you mean by nothing."

"She knows I love my daughter and I . . . I was . . . uh . . ."

"Yes?"

"Just that I love her, that's all."

64

"What does '*I know what you're trying to do*' mean?"

"I think she was referring to my trying to see Monica more often," Boone said.

"Is that why she feels she should '*harbor ill will*'?" Kling asked.

"Hmh? Is that what she said?"

"Read the letter," Kling said, extending it.

"No, I believe you." Boone shrugged. "I don't know what she means by that."

"No inkling, huh?"

"Nope."

"Um-huh. How about this letter she says she received. Know anything about it?"

"Not a thing."

"When did you leave for Connecticut?"

"Friday morning. The 7th."

"What time?"

"I left here at about eight."

"Why?"

"A client. Some portrait work."

"And you planned to work over the weekend, is that right?"

"Yes."

"When did you plan on returning?"

"I planned to be back at the studio on Monday morning."

"Were you?"

"No."

"When did you get back?"

"I got into the city at about eleven Monday night."

"The night Annie was killed."

"Yes."

"Did you call your office?"

"At eleven P.M.?"

"I suppose not. Were there any messages for you at the switchboard here?"

"Yes. Annie had called."

"Did you call her back?"

"No."

"Why not?"

"I figured whatever it was could wait until morning. I was awfully tired, Mr. Kling."

"But you didn't try to reach her the next morning."

"I'd seen the papers by then. I knew she was dead."

"Okay. I'll take this letter with me, if you don't mind. It may help us."

"Go right ahead," Boone said. He looked at Kling levelly. "You still think I had something to do with this?"

"Let's say there are certain contradictions present, Mr. Boone."

"What time was Annie killed?" Boone asked.

"Coroner says about ten-thirty," Kling said.

"Then I'm out of it."

"Why? Because you say you didn't get back to the city until eleven?"

"No. Because I was in a diner from ten to ten-thirty. The owner was interested in photography. We had a long chat."

"Which diner?"

"It's called The Hub. It's forty miles from the city. I couldn't have killed her. Check it. The man'll remember me. I gave him my card."

"Forty miles from the city?" Kling asked.

"Forty miles. On Route 38. Check it."

"I will," Kling said. He rose and walked to the door. At the door, he turned. "Mr. Boone?" he said.

"Yes?"

"In the meantime, don't go to Connecticut this weekend."

The law offices of Jefferson Dobberly were straight out of *Great Expectations*. They were small and musty, and they received rays of slanted sunlight upon which dust motes floated. Enormous legal tomes lined the reception room, lined the corridor leading to Dobberly's private office, and lined three walls of the private office itself.

Jefferson Dobberly sat before the windows which lined the fourth wall. Sunlight slanted in behind his balding head. Dust motes danced on the sunlight and on his pate. Books were piled on his desk, and they formed a fortress between him and Kling. Kling sat and watched him. He was a tall thin man with watery blue eyes. His mouth was wrinkled and he moved it perpetually, as if he wanted to spit and couldn't find a place to do it. He had cut himself shaving that morning. The gash ran sidewards on his cheek from his left sideburn. The sideburns were practically all that remained of the hair on his head, and even they were white as if they were weakening before their final surrender. Jefferson Dobberly was fifty-three years old. He looked like seventy.

"What has Theodore Boone done in connection with getting custody of his daughter Monica?" Kling asked.

"I don't see what bearing that has on the case you're investigating, Mr. Kling," Dobberly said. His voice, in complete contradiction to his fragile appearance, was loud and booming. He spoke as if he were addressing a jury. He spoke as if every word he uttered were the key word in his summing up.

"*You* don't have to see the bearing, Mr. Dobberly," Kling said gently. "Only the police do."

Dobberly smiled.

"Will you tell me, sir?" Kling asked.

"What did Mr. Boone tell you?"

"Counsellor," Kling said gently, and Dobberly reared back slightly at the word, "this is a murder investigation. Let's not play footsie."

"Well, Mr. Kling," Dobberly said, still smiling, and Kling repeated, "This is a *murder* investigation," and the smile left Dobberly's face.

"What do you want to know?" Dobberly asked.

"What's he doing to get his child?"

"Now?"

"Yes, now."

"Mrs. Travail refuses to release the child. Under the law, Ted . . . Mr. Boone can take forcible possession of her. He prefers not to handle it that way. For the child's sake. We have asked instead for an *ex parte* court order. We may have it any time within the next week or so. That's it."

"When did you apply for the court order?"

"The day after Annie was killed."

"Had Mr. Boone made any prior attempts to gain custody of the child?" Kling asked.

Dobberly hesitated.

"Had he?"

"Well, they've been divorced for almost two years, you know."

"Yes."

"I had handled Ted's law affairs before that. When they

decided to get a divorce, they naturally came to me. I tried to prevent it. But . . . well, people have their own reasons, I guess. Annie went to Las Vegas."

"Go on."

"Ted came to me about six months later. He said he wanted Monica."

"You told him the courts had awarded the child to Annie, and that was that. Am I right?"

"Well, no, not exactly. That's not exactly what I told him."

"What did you tell him?"

"I told him that the courts have been known to reverse their decision regarding custody. If, for example, the mother is shown to be unfit."

"How do you mean?"

"Unfit, Mr. Kling. If, for example, she is raising the child in a house of prostitution. Or if, for example, it is shown that she is a drug addict, or an alcoholic."

"But this was not the case with Annie."

"Well . . ." Dobberly hesitated.

"Well?"

"Mr. Kling, I always liked Annie. I don't like to talk against her. I'm telling you this only because my client felt he could base a case upon it. When we made our appeal . . ."

"You made an appeal?"

"Yes. In an attempt to get a reversal of decision."

"When was this?"

"We entered the appeal almost a year ago."

"What happened?"

Dobberly shrugged. "Court calendars are jammed, Mr. Kling. We were still waiting when Annie was killed. I have withdrawn the appeal. There is no need for it now. Mr. Boone has the legal right to that child now."

"This appeal," Kling said. "On what was it based?"

"We were trying to show that Annie was an unfit mother. You must understand, Mr. Kling, that if she failed to dress the child properly, or if they lived in a poor neighborhood, or if she had too many . . : ah . . . boy friends . . . well, none of these would be sufficient reasons to support a claim of unfitness. You understand that."

"Yes," Kling said. "What was unfit about Annie?"

Dobberly sighed heavily. "She was a hopeless drunkard," he said.

"Boone never mentioned that," Kling said. "Neither did her mother." Kling thought a moment. "Did this have any connection with the fact that she worked in a liquor store?"

"Perhaps. I haven't seen Annie since the divorce. She was *not* a drunkard then."

"Then she became one between the time of the divorce and the time you made your appeal, is that right?"

"Apparently. Yes. Unless her alcoholism was kept secret during the time I knew her. I wouldn't know about that."

"You know Boone well, am I right?"

"Fairly well, yes."

"He told me he made no attempt to see either Annie or the child until six months after the divorce. Yet he claims he loved both very much. Can you offer any explanation for his behavior?"

"Certainly," Dobberly said.

"What?"

"He was hoping he'd get her back. Annie, I mean. He stayed away from her and the child because he thought she'd miss him, thought she'd want him again, thought she'd 'come to her senses,' as he put it." Dobberly shrugged sadly. "It didn't work that way, Mr. Kling. And finally, Ted faced the facts. It was all over. That was when he decided he wanted Monica. If he couldn't have Annie, he would at least have the child. That's the way his thinking went, Mr. Kling."

"I see. Have you ever met Mrs. Travail?"

"Ted's mother-in-law? Never. From what he says about her, she seems to be the mother-in-law who's in all the nasty jokes one hears."

"She speaks very highly of him."

"Does she?" Dobberly raised his eyebrows. "I'm surprised."

"Why?"

"Well, as I said, Ted seems to dislike her intensely." Dobberly paused. "You don't seriously believe he killed Annie, do you?"

"I don't seriously believe anything yet," Kling said.

"He didn't kill that girl, Mr. Kling, believe me. I'm

willing to bet my life on that. The boy's harmless. Annie Boone took a lot of happiness out of his life. He was only trying to recapture a little of it by getting his daughter back. He would no more do murder than you or I."

"*I* would, Mr. Dobberly," Kling said.

"In the line of duty, yes. Legal murder. If you had to. But Ted Boone didn't have to."

"How else would he have gotten his daughter back?"

"I already told you, Mr. Kling. Annie was a drunkard."

"I have only your word for that, so far. And you admitted you hadn't seen her since the divorce. I hardly think you'd make a capable witness as to whether or not she was a drunkard."

"Ted can tell you," Dobberly said.

"If Ted Boone committed murder, he can tell me a lot of things, all of which might be untrue."

"He's not a criminal type. I used to be a criminal lawyer many years ago, when I first began practice. Those were booming days for criminals. I was very busy. I got to know criminal types. Surely, Mr. Kling, you are familiar with criminal types."

"Surely, Mr. Dobberly, you are familiar with the fact that most murders are not committed by people with previous criminal records."

"Yes. But I do not feel that Ted Boone is capable of murder."

"I hope you're right. What kind of a girl was Annie?"

"Pretty, vibrant."

"Overly intelligent?"

"Average, I would say."

"Overly quick?"

Dobberly shrugged. "Average."

"Would you say she had outgrown Mr. Boone?"

"No, I don't think so. They both seemed to have grown in social experience. Naturally, I didn't have very much to do with them. That is, I only saw them occasionally. Whenever Ted needed the services of an attorney. It was Anne, you know, who wanted the divorce. Ted didn't. I tried to keep them together. I always do. But she wanted it. It was a strange thing. They seemed very well matched."

"But you didn't see them very often?"

"No."

"How often?"

"In the two years I'd known them before the divorce? Oh, perhaps a dozen times." Dobberly shook his head. "Very well matched. I couldn't understand it. I tried to keep them together. But she wanted the divorce. I still don't know why."

"There's only one person who does, Mr. Dobberly," Kling said.

"Who?"

"Annie Boone."

CHAPTER 8

REGAL OLDSMOBILE was in that part of the city called Riverhead. There was, in actuality, no river which had its head—or even its tail—in that part of the city. In the days of the old Dutch settlers the entire part of the city above Isola was owned by a patroon named Ryerhert. Ryerhert's Farms was good land interspersed with igneous and metamorphic rock. As the city grew, Ryerhert sold part of his land and donated the rest of it until eventually all of it was owned by the city. Ryerhert was hard to say. Even before 1917 when it became unfashionable for anything to sound even mildly Teutonic, Ryerhert had become Riverhead. There was, to be sure, water in Riverhead. But the water was a brook, really, and it wasn't even called a brook. It was called Five Mile Pond. It was not five miles wide, nor was it five miles long, nor was it five miles from any noticeable landmark. It was simply a brook which was called Five Mile Pond in a community called Riverhead which had no river's head in it. Riverhead could get confusing sometimes.

Regal Oldsmobile was in the heart of Riverhead on an avenue called Barbara Avenue beneath the elevated structure. Regal Oldsmobile was composed of two branches, or rather three. It was easy to make the error of thinking there were only two departments because there were only two buildings. But one of those buildings housed the new cars showroom and the service department. The other building housed the used cars department. Two buildings, three branches. Very confusing. Like Riverhead itself.

Detectives Cotton Hawes and Steve Carella were primarily interested in the service department of Regal Oldsmobile. They spoke there with a man named Buck

Mosley. Buck was covered with oil. He had been engaged in changing a differential when the detectives arrived. Buck didn't like to talk much, anyway. He was good with his hands, and the other mechanics felt he did most of his talking to cars, but they never begrudged him the title of Service Manager because they knew he was the best damned mechanic at Regal. It isn't everyone who can talk to an automobile. And even fewer people can get an answer from one. Buck could do both these things. With people, it was different. With people, he was somewhat reticent. With people who also happened to be cops, Buck somehow resembled the lowly clam.

"It was you who called us in answer to our flyer, wasn't it?" Hawes asked.

"Uh-huh," Buck said.

"You think your department did the paint job on the '47 Dodge?"

"Uh-huh."

"What color did you paint it?"

"Green," Buck said.

"What kind of green?"

"Kelly."

"Bright?"

"Uh-huh."

"When was this?"

"Three weeks ago," Buck said in a longish sentence which qualified him as a marathon lecturer.

"For whom?"

"Fellow."

"Do you know his name?"

"Inside," Buck said, gesturing to the office with his head. He began walking. Hawes and Carella followed him.

"Don't let him talk too much," Carella whispered. "Tire the poor fellow out."

Hawes grinned. "Uh-huh," he said.

In the office, Buck did not speak until he found the service record. Then he extended it to Carella and said only, "Here."

Carella looked at the form.

"Charles Fetterick," Carella said. "Ever see him before?"

"Nope," Buck said.

"Just came in off the street?" Hawes asked.

REGAL OLDSMOBILE, INC.
NEW AND USED CARS
Sales and Service
4850 Barbara Avenue
Riverhead

Tel. SA 5-6321

Name: Charles Fetterick
Address: 127 Boxer Lane
City: Riverhead   Phone: AK 2-1049

Make: Dodge   Type or Model: Sedan   Year: 1947

Operation No.:   Date: 5/27

REPAIR ORDER INSTRUCTIONS	Labor charge
Check distributor	2 50
Replace points & condenser	
Replace resistor	62 00
Repaint	64 50

MATERIAL USED

Quan.	Part No.	Parts	Price
1	Set points		1 80
1	Condenser		95
1	Resistor		1 55
2	Gallons Green Paint		10 20

PHONE WHEN READY?   YES ☒   NO ☐

BROUGHT FORWARD   14 60

"Yep."

"Car been in a smackup?"

"Nope."

"Stolen?"

"Checked the list," Buck said loquaciously. "Okay."

"Just wanted it repainted," Hawes said. "That's strange."

"It may have been spotted on another heist," Carella

74

<table>
<tr><td>ORDER TAKEN BY:</td><td>Buddha</td></tr>
<tr><td>LICENSE NO.:</td><td>PC 485Y</td></tr>
<tr><td>SER. NO.:</td><td>XY 1012-14-21</td></tr>
<tr><td>MOTOR NO.:</td><td>V 4221-701</td></tr>
</table>

NOT RESPONSIBLE FOR LOSS OR DAMAGE TO CARS OR ARTICLES LEFT IN CARS IN CASE OF FIRE, THEFT OR ANY OTHER CAUSE BEYOND OUR CONTROL.

GAS, OIL AND GREASE	PRICE
10 GALS. GAS @ 21	2-10
QTS. OIL @	
LBS. GREASE @	
TOTAL GAS, OIL AND GREASE	2-10
TOTAL LABOR	64 50
TOTAL PARTS	14 60
ACCESSORIES	
OUTSIDE REPAIR	
TAX	2 44
TOTAL AMOUNT	83 64

I hereby authorize the above repair work to be done with the necessary material and hereby grant to Regal Oldsmobile and its employees permission to operate the car or truck herein described on streets, highways or elsewhere for the purpose of testing and/or inspection. An express mechanic's lien is hereby acknowledged on above car or truck to secure the amount of repairs thereto.

x Charles R. Fetterick

NO. 213-46-8750
Form DL 46
Manufactured by Alco Press, Inc. Isola.

said. He looked at the form again. "127 Boxer. That isn't far. Let's make the collar."

"Shouldn't we run him through the I.B. first?"

"What for?"

"I like to know what I'm going against," Hawes said.

"By the time we check on whether or not he's got a record, he may have moved to California," Carella said.

"Let's nab him while we know where he is. *If* this is the real address."

"Whatever you say," Hawes said. He turned to Buck. "Thanks a lot," he told him.

"Welcome," Buck said, and that was that.

It was by the sheerest good fortune that Steve Carella remained alive that day. When it was all over, he had only Cotton Hawes to thank for his close brush with the black angel. When it was all over, he was in no mood to thank Cotton Hawes. He said, instead, "You stupid son of a bitch!" even though Hawes got his share of the lumps and was lying flat on his back in a tenement hallway.

They had left Regal Oldsmobile at ten minutes to noon. Hawes wanted to stop for lunch. Carella wanted to nab Fetterick. Hawes conceded.

The tenements lining Boxer Lane were perhaps better tenements than those to be found in the 87th Precinct territory. The ones in the 87th were generally cold water railroad flats heated by kerosene stoves. The kerosene stoves accounted for the fact that the fire house in the 87th was the most overworked house in the city, answering some 2500 calls yearly, with the heaviest load in the winter. The tenements on Boxer Lane all had steam heat. Aside from that, the line between them and the 87th's tenements was a thin one. Tenements are tenements.

Cops, too, are cops. They are used to tenements. They are used to entering dimly lit entrance hallways and seeing broken mailboxes. They are used to garbage cans stacked on the ground floor, and narrow steps leading to each landing of the multiple dwelling. They are used to the smells of a tenement and the sounds of a tenement. The tenement in which Charles Fetterick, Thief, lived was no different from any other tenement in the world. Charles Fetterick, Thief, had his name in a broken mailbox. The apartment number lettered on the small white card was 34. Cotton Hawes and Steve Carella, Detectives, began climbing the steps to the third floor in hope of apprehending Charles Fetterick, Thief.

They passed an old man on the second floor. The old man knew they were bulls. He could tell simply by looking at them. He stood on the second floor landing and looked up after them curiously, wondering whom they were after.

On the third floor landing, Carella drew his service revolver. Hawes studied him dispassionately for a moment and then drew this own .38. He heard Carella click off the safety. He followed suit. In the dimness of the corridor, they found Apartment 34. Carella put his ear to the door. There was no sound from within the apartment. He backed away from the door and leaned momentarily against the opposite wall, preparatory to shoving himself off the wall and kicking out at the lock with the flat of his left foot. He was remembering that Charles Fetterick was perhaps the fellow who'd thrown Roger Havilland through a plate glass window and killed him. He was remembering that Roger Havilland wasn't exactly a half pint, and that it must have taken quite a shove to brush him off into that window. He was remembering, too, that he had a lovely wife named Teddy, and he had no intention of leaving her a young widow. And so his .38 was cocked and ready in his right fist, and he backed off onto the opposite wall preparatory to kicking in a door lock, an operation he had performed perhaps fifty thousand or sixty thousand or sixty million times since he'd been a cop, a very simple and routine operation, a thing as common as answering the phone with "87th Squad, Detective Carella."

When Hawes knocked on the door, Carella blinked.

When Hawes said, without waiting for an answer to his knock, "Police, Fetterick. Open up!" Carella was speechless. He still would have kicked in the lock, except that a series of explosions sounded from within the apartment, and suddenly the wood of the door was splintering outward and bullets were whizzing past Carella's head and knocking big chunks of plaster from the wall. He didn't think anything then but *DUCK!* He fell flat to the floor with his pistol in his fist, and then the door opened and Charles Fetterick—or whoever the hell was inside the apartment—threw another shot out of the doorjamb, and Hawes stood with his mouth wide open and Fetterick—or whoever the hell was shoving his way out of the door—slammed his gun sidewards against Hawes' head without saying a word. Hawes brought up his hand to cover the wide gash of blood that suddenly crossed his eye and Fet-

77

terick—or whoever the hell was wielding that gun—lashed out at Hawes again, opening his nose and sending him sprawling backwards against Carella who hugged the floor and who was angling for a shot past the six-foot-two-inch bulk of Hawes. Hawes came down. He came down onto Carella's right hand, pinning the gun. Fetterick—or whoever the hell was wearing those size twelve shoes—kicked out at Hawes' face, splitting his lip, and then he ran for the steps. By the time Carella rolled Hawes off him and onto his back, Fetterick was in the street and probably eight blocks away. Carella walked back to Hawes. There were four shots in the plaster where Carella's head had once been. Hawes lay on the floor with his face open at every seam.

"You stupid son of a bitch!" Carella said. "Are you all right?"

CHAPTER 9

WHEN A NEW man joins a firm, the other employees are apt to talk about him, speculate about him, generally form their own conclusions about him. If he contributes something colorful to the working day, the employees very often will take their talk home to their wives. They will dissect the newcomer at the dinner table.

Cops are only employees of the city. Cotton Hawes had contributed a most colorful tidbit to the working day, and so that night . . .

"All right, so he's polite," Meyer Meyer said to his wife as he sliced the steak. "This I can understand. A man is polite, he's polite. You can't separate a man from good manners that have been bred into him, am I right?"

Sarah Meyer nodded and spooned mashed potatoes onto the plates of the three Meyer children. She was a woman of thirty-four, with brown hair and eyes as blue as Meyer's. Around the table, Alan, Susie, and Jeff sat, three miniature blue-eyed reproductions of their parents.

"But now politeness," Meyer said, putting the first slice of steak onto Sarah's plate, "is a thing you have to be careful about." He put the second slice of steak onto Susie's plate, and then served the boys. He served himself last. The children bowed their heads and clasped their hands. Meyer bowed his head and said, "Thank you, dear Lord, for providing." He picked up his fork. "It may be polite to knock on a door and say, 'Excuse me, sir, this is the police. Would you be so kind as to open up?' This may be considered very polite in the 30th Precinct. Maybe in the 30th Precinct, they got butlers to open the doors for cheap thieves. Maybe that's the way it works there."

"Did Steve get shot?" Sarah asked.

"No," Meyer said. "Thank God, he didn't get shot. But that is not this Cotton Hawes' fault. Hawes was doing his polite best, you can bank on that." Meyer nodded emphatically.

"Cotton is a stupid name, anyway," Jeff, who was eight, said.

"Nobody asked you," Meyer told him. "Steve could have got his head blown off. He's lucky he didn't get it at least creased. Would you pass the green beans, please, Sarah darling?"

Sarah passed the green beans.

"He knocked on the door! Can you imagine that? He actually knocked on the door."

"Ain't you *supposed* to knock on doors, Pop?" Alan, who was eleven, asked.

"Aren't," Sarah corrected.

"Yeah, aren't?" Alan said.

"If you come to our bedroom," Meyer said judiciously, "and the door is closed, certainly you should knock. That's manners. Or even if you're visiting outside, and you come to a closed door, you should knock, certainly. That, too, is manners. We are not discussing *your* manners, Alan; or yours, Susie; or yours, Jeff."

"Then whose?" Susie, who was ten, asked.

"We are discussing the manners of the police department," Meyer said. "And the best police department is the one which has hardly any manners at all."

"Meyer," Sarah warned. "The children."

"We already separated children from cops," Meyer said. "Would you pass me a roll, please? Besides, the children know that what's said in this house is family stuff and doesn't go beyond these four walls. Am I right, children?"

"Yes, Pop," Jeff said.

Susie and Alan nodded as if Meyer had just entrusted them with the plans for the new atomic submarine. Meyer looked around the table for the butter.

"What's with this kosher bit?" he asked. "Get me some butter, will you, darling, please?"

Sarah rose from the table, grinning. "You're a heathen," she said gently.

"I'm a heathen," Meyer said, shrugging. "I'm a cop. I got to keep up my strength. Who knows, some day I'll be out on a squeal with Mr. Cotton, and we'll capture a criminal wanted in twenty states, and Mr. Cotton will hand him his gun and say, 'Hold this for me a minute, will you?' For this, you need strength."

"He shouldn't have knocked, Daddy?" Susie asked.

"Darling," Meyer said, "the man in that apartment was wanted for murder. With a man who is wanted for murder, the only knocking you do is on his head."

Susie giggled, and from the kitchen Sarah said, "Meyer!"

"I should teach them to be kind to murderers?"

Sarah came back into the dining room. "That isn't it," she said. "You shouldn't joke about hitting people on the head."

"All right, it's no joke," Meyer admitted. "The only joke around is Cotton Hawes. You should see him. He was bleeding from a hundred holes."

"Meyer!" Sarah said sharply.

"Well, he was! Do you want me to say he *wasn't* bleeding from a hundred holes?"

"We happen to be eating."

"I know. This is good steak. He had to go to the hospital. Nothing serious, but they bandaged him up like the invisible man. Crazy. He brought it on himself. Knocking! My God."

"Was Steve angry?"

"I don't know. He wasn't saying much. This Mr. Cotton should have calling cards printed. It should say on them 'Cotton Hawes Calling.' He should knock and then slide one under the door. I'll bet he lasts three days if he keeps knocking on doors. We'll be identifying him from something they drag out of the River Dix."

"Meyer!"

"All right, all right, already," Meyer said. He smiled ingratiatingly. "Pass the salt, please, darling, would you please, Sarah darling?"

Lieutenant Peter Byrnes sat at the dinner table with his wife Harriet and his son Larry. He was a compact man, Byrnes, with a compact bullet head. He had tiny blue eyes set in a seamed and weathered face which was divided by a craggy nose. His upper lip was a little weak, but his lower lip was strong and pouting, and he owned a chin like a cleft boulder. His head sat snugly on his short, thick neck,

81

as if he were ready to pull it in at a moment's notice. His hands were thick hands belonging to an honest man who had worked hard all his life.

He sat at the table emanating silence, and Harriet watched him. The only sound in the room was the sound of eighteen-year-old Larry wolfing his food.

"All right," Harriet said at last. "What is it?"

"I like Steve Carella," Byrnes said. "I mean it. I liked that boy. By Christ, when we almost lost him last Christmas . . ."

"Did he do something wrong?" Harriet asked.

"No, he didn't do anything wrong," Byrnes said, shaking his head. "No, it isn't him. I'm just saying I like him, and I like his wife. I look at that girl as if she's my own daughter. I swear it. A man who runs a squad isn't supposed to have favorites, but I like that boy. He's a damned fine boy."

Larry Byrnes said nothing. He ate with the complete abandon of a hungry adolescent. It had not been so long ago that Larry Byrnes' hunger had not been for the normal adolescent pleasures. He had not forgotten that Steve Carella had been shot trying to solve a narcotics case in which he'd been involved. That was all behind them now, a part of the Byrnes existence they no longer discussed, but he had not forgotten. He knew why his father's favorite cop was Steve Carella. His own favorite cop, since last Christmas, was a detective-lieutenant named Peter Byrnes. So he listened to his father attentively, but he nonetheless managed to gobble his food with total adolescent oblivion.

"I like Steve, too," Harriet said. "What happened?"

"He almost got killed today," Byrnes said.

"What!"

"Yes, yes. Four bullets that missed him by maybe half an inch."

"Steve? How?"

"Hawes," Byrnes said. "Cotton Hawes. They had to send him to me. Of all the precincts in the city, they had to pick mine. They take him out of a precinct which is a finishing school for young girls, and they send him to the 87th. The 87th! Of all the precincts! What did I do to deserve him? What did I do to deserve a man who knocks on a murderer's door and announces that the police are there?"

"Is that what he did?" Harriet asked, astonished.

"That's what he did."

"What happened?"

"The guy opened fire. Almost ripped Steve's head off. Hawes got himself beat to a pulp. What am I gonna do with him? Put him on tracing lost bicycles? I need all the cops I can get. Havilland may have been a terrible guy personally, but he wasn't a bad cop. He really wasn't, Harriet. Loose with his hands, yes, and I don't go for that. But he wasn't a bad cop. He didn't pull stupid blunders. I can't afford to risk a man like Steve Carella because of a stupid blunder a jerk like Cotton Hawes makes!"

"The one who fired? Is he the man who killed Roger?"

"We think so."

"And this Hawes *knocked* on the door?"

"Yes! Can you believe it? Harriet, tell me the God's honest truth. Would *you* have knocked on that door?"

"I'd have kicked it in," Harriet said calmly, "and shot at the first thing that moved."

"Good," Byrnes said. "Would you like to join my squad?"

"I joined it the day we were married," Harriet said, smiling.

Byrnes smiled, too. He looked at Larry. He sighed heavily.

"Son," he said, "I know a famine is expected this year, but go easy. We've been hoarding food in the basement."

In the living room of Claire Townsend's apartment, she and Detective Bert Kling were necking.

It was a pleasant spot to neck, much more comfortable than the back seat of an automobile. Ralph Townsend, Claire's father, had retired at 10:30, leaving the living room to "the kids," figuring that nothing very terrible or spectacular could happen to two people who were already engaged. On that particular night, he was absolutely right because Bert Kling didn't have his mind on necking somehow. The lights were dimmed and there was soft music coming from the record player, but all Kling could do was talk about Cotton Hawes.

"Knocks on the door," he said. "This is me, Renfrew of the Mounted! Bang! Four shots come plowing through the wood. Steve almost collected his life insurance."

"Are we going to talk about Cotton Hawes all night?"

"He's a danger," Kling said. "He's a positive danger. I hope to hell I never answer a squeal with him."

"He's new. He'll learn."

"When? When all the cops on the squad are dead? Oh, Claire, this man is dangerous."

"I wish *you* were a little more dangerous."

"How do you mean?"

"You figure it out."

"Oh," Kling said. He kissed her perfunctorily. "But how can a man be so ignorant?" he persisted. "How can a man deliberately . . . ?"

"Is it considered impolite for policemen to knock on doors?"

"It's considered wonderful," Kling said. "Except when the man in the apartment is a suspected murderer."

"This man was a suspected murderer?"

"This man was the man who threw Roger Havilland into the plate glass window."

"Oh."

"So would you have knocked?"

"I'd have said 'Kiss me, lover,'" Claire said.

"What?"

"Kiss me, lover," she repeated.

So he kissed her.

The only man who wasn't doing much complaining was Steve Carella. At home with Teddy, he had more important things on his mind. He did not like taking police work home with him. He saw too many things during the day which often left him feeling sick. He knew too many cops who had allowed the filth of criminal detection to wipe off on the floor mats of their homes. Teddy was a sweet girl, Teddy was his wife. Except when something was really troubling him, except when there was a nut too difficult to crack, he did not usually discuss the precinct or the squad with her. Besides, what had happened this afternoon was over and done with. It had been close, but he'd survived in one piece, and maybe Hawes had learned a lesson. The lesson undoubtedly would have been driven home with sharper impact had Carella been killed. Unfortunately, he had not. Hawes would have to derive from the lesson what he could —without the benefit of homicide.

Steve Carella kissed his wife. She was good to kiss. She was a brunette with brown eyes and full lips and a full body, and he enjoyed kissing her. The room was very quiet, dark except where the street lamps below filtered up to the open windows. Steve Carella didn't tell Teddy about Hawes.

Steve Carella had more important things on his mind.

CHAPTER 10

ON BOXER LANE, there walked a man who felt like a horse's ass.

The man had adhesive tape all over his face. The man was six feet two inches tall and weighed one hundred and ninety pounds. He had blue eyes and a square jaw with a cleft chin. His hair was red, except for a streak over his left temple where he had once been knifed and where the hair had curiously grown in white after the wound healed.

The man's name was Cotton Hawes.

The man was off duty, but he had nonetheless come back to Boxer Lane because he wanted to find out more about the man who'd thrown four slugs through the door and then beaten him silly. His pride was injured and his face was injured, but most of all he felt pretty stupid. He did not like to feel stupid. He'd have felt even more stupid had Carella been killed. He thought again of the absurdity of his knocking, thought again of those four shocking explosions which had sent Carella plummeting to the floor. *Carella could be dead now,* he thought. *I could have killed Carella this afternoon.*

The thought was not a pleasant one. For perhaps Hawes was an opinionated man, and perhaps he'd been raised on a squad where murderers were not too frequent guests, and perhaps he was impatient, and perhaps he was somewhat snide and disrespectful at times, but he thought highly of his profession, and he had a heart as wide as the Grand Canyon. He would no more have wanted Steve Carella dead than he'd have wanted himself dead. Nor had he wanted to commit such a stupid blunder that afternoon. He supposed he'd been too eager. He hadn't stopped to think. Failure to think was a bad habit for a cop to develop, especially in a precinct like the 87th. It was becoming increasingly clear to Hawes that the 87th was a little bit different from anything he'd come across in his years on the force. Curiously, he enjoyed the challenge. He was a cop because he wanted to fight crime. There had been crime in the 30th, to be sure, but the crime there when compared to the crime in the 87th was somewhat like a glass of ginger ale set alongside a vodka martini.

Hawes had the feeling he could learn a lot in the 87th. He had the further feeling that Steve Carella was the man to teach him. He never would have given Carella the satisfaction of knowing it, but it was what he thought nonetheless. Naturally, his blunder that afternoon was not the sort of thing which endeared man to man, or so he thought. He did not know that Carella had already chalked off the incident. Had he known Carella, Hawes also would have known he was not a man to harbor grudges. He did not know Carella. He himself was at that stage of maturity where harboring grudges seemed like the right thing to do. And so, using his own personality as a sounding board, he automatically assumed that Carella would be harboring a grudge for what had happened that afternoon.

At the same time, it was important to Hawes that Carella like him. He knew that Carella was a good cop and an intelligent man. His instinct had told him that much. He wanted to learn from the good cop, and be liked by the intelligent man. It was as simple as that. But he could do neither if Carella looked upon him as an idiot.

This was the reasoning which had brought him to Boxer Lane that evening of June 15th. It was a Saturday night, and a young man of thirty-two conceivably could have found something more entertaining to do on a Saturday night—but Hawes, in his own mind, had a blunder to eradicate.

He had, in a sense, compounded his own felony that afternoon. Immediately after the shooting, Carella had insisted upon getting him to a hospital. He had flatly refused. He realized now that his refusal had been only an extension of his original stupidity. He had been in no condition to search an apartment, and he did not imagine that a man like Carella appreciated petty heroics. They had gone over the room for ten minutes when Carella came over to him.

"Look, Hawes," he'd said, "you're bleeding badly. If I

87

have to knock you out and personally carry you to the hospital, I'll do it. Do I have to knock you out?"

Hawes had sheepishly shaken his head, and Carella had driven him to the hospital. As a result, they had not got around to questioning any of the tenants. Hawes hoped to accomplish that tonight.

He found the superintendent in a basement room. The super was sprawled out face downward on a cot. The small room stank of whiskey fumes. Hawes went to the cot and shook him. The old man rolled over.

"Whuzzit?" he said. "Whoozzit?"

"Police," Hawes said. "Wake up."

The old man sat up and rubbed his eyes sleepily. "Whuddyawant?" he asked.

"Answers," Hawes said.

"Whudtime'zit?" the old man asked.

"Eight-thirty."

"Too early to get up. Too early in the morning."

"It's night. How long did Charles Fetterick live here?" Hawes asked.

"Lemme see your badge," the super said.

"I was here this afternoon," Hawes said. He flipped open his wallet to where his shield was pinned to the leather. "Are you sober?"

"I'm soberezza judge," the super said.

"Can you understand me?"

"Sure."

"Can you answer me?"

"Sure."

"How long did Fetterick live here?"

"Month, two months. About that. He do something? Hey, heeeeey!"

"What is it?"

The super pointed a bony finger at Hawes' face. "You're the cop he beat up this afternoon, ain't you?"

"Yes," Hawes admitted.

"Then he sure *did* do something, huh?"

"He did worse than that," Hawes said.

"What?"

"Nothing. Did he have any friends in the building?"

"I don't know. I don't bother with the tenants much. I make the steam, fix the plumbing, the electricity, stuff like

88

that. I don't socialize much. I'm what you call a non-mixer. I'm what you call a professional non-joiner."

"Fetterick married?"

"Nope."

"Notice him here with girls?"

"Girls?"

"Girls."

The super shrugged. "Never did notice. Long as a man doesn't bang on the pipes for heat, I don't much care what he does in his own apartment. I don't own this building. I just make the steam, fix the plumb . . ."

"Yes, I know."

"You might ask some of the tenants on his floor. They might know. Me, I don't socialize much. I'm what you call a non . . ."

"I know," Hawes said. "Thanks a lot."

"Glad to be of assistance," the old man said. He lay down and rolled over as Hawes left the room.

Hawes climbed to the third floor and knocked on Apartment 31. He knocked again. There was no answer. He kept knocking. A door opened. It was not the door upon which he knocked. It was the door to Apartment 32 next door. A girl stood in the doorway.

"They aren't home," she said.

The girl wore black slacks and a black sweater. Her blond hair was pulled back into a pony tail. At first glance, she seemed out of place in the tenement doorway, too chic, too sophisticated. She should have been standing in the entrance doorway to a penthouse, holding a martini.

"I'm a cop," Hawes said, "Mind if I ask *you* a few questions?"

"You were knockin' on 31," the girl said. "This is 32."

"I'm really interested in 34," Hawes said.

"What cup?" the girl asked, and Hawes didn't get it. She looked at him glumly. "This about Fetterick?" she asked, apparently deciding to play it straight.

"Yes."

"Come on in."

Hawes followed her into the apartment. It was then that he noticed the black sweater was worn through at the elbows. The girl flicked on a light. "Want a drink?" she asked.

"No, thanks."

"What a drag, huh? Saturday night, and no date."

"Yeah," Hawes said. "About Fetterick . . ."

"A jerk," the girl said, shrugging.

"You knew him?"

The girl shrugged again. "Only to talk to. We took in the milk together, so to speak. Whenever it wasn't stolen."

"What was he like?"

"A jerk," the girl said, "like I told you. Inferiority complex. Probably wanted to sleep with his mother when he was a kid. Like that."

"Huh?" Hawes said.

"Oedipus," the girl said. "Aggravated. Made him feel inferior. His father was a big man. He never could shape up to the fact."

"You got all this taking in the milk?" Hawes asked, astonished.

"I figured it out for myself. I'm speculating," the girl said. "What'd he do?"

"We think he killed a cop."

"Oh. Too bad for him, huh? You guys'll beat the crap outa him when you get him."

"Who said?"

"Everybody knows that. Cop killer? Boom! Right on his dome. How old are you?"

"Thirty-two."

"That's a good age. You married?"

"No."

"Mmm," the girl said, and she looked at him speculatively.

"Oedipus," Hawes said. "Aggravated."

"Huh? Oh." The girl grinned. "Humor on a cop. Wonders never cease. You sure you don't want a drink?"

"I'm sure," Hawes said.

"I'll have one," the girl said. "My name's Jenny. Jenny Pelenco. Euphemistic, huh?"

"Very," Hawes said, smiling.

"Saturday night, no date. What a drag. Jesus!" She went to the sink and poured herself a shot of rye. "I think I'll get crocked. Get crocked with me?"

"No, thanks."

"What are you scared of?" the girl asked. "My husband's in the Navy."

"Where?"

"Far enough," she said, laughing. "The Pacific."

"What about Fetterick?"

"Who wants to get crocked with him?"

"I didn't mean that. What do you know about him?"

"What do you want to know? Ask Jenny Pelenco. I'm the barber's wife. That's an Italian expression. It means like the barber's wife knows everything goes on in town because she hears it from the barber. You get it?"

"Vaguely. Know what kind of work Fetterick did?"

"No. He never said. A bum, I think."

"Ever see him leave the house with gloves?"

"Yeah. Hey, yeah. Is that important?"

"Not very. He never mentioned his job?"

"No. I figure him for either a bum or something very low. Like a ditch digger. Or a bricklayer."

"Those are both honest jobs," Hawes said.

"So? Honest makes them good? A bricklayer is a jerk. Fetterick is a jerk, so he must be a bricklayer."

"He never said where he worked?"

"No."

"Did you ever see him leaving for work in the morning?"

"Yeah."

"What time?"

"Eight, eight-thirty."

"Did he work in Riverhead?"

"Beats me. Mind if I have another drink?"

"Go right ahead. Did you ever notice any of his friends? People who came or went to the apartment?"

"He was a lone wolf," Jenny said. She tossed off the shot. "I better go easy," she said, grinning. "I get wild when I'm crocked."

"Mmm," Hawes said.

"I get the urge when I'm crocked," she said, still grinning.

"Then you'd better go easy," Hawes said. "Anything else you can tell me about Fetterick?"

"No. A jerk. A bum. A bricklayer. Common. I invited him in for a drink once. He refused. A jerk, huh?"

"Did he have any girl friends?"

"None that I saw. A jerk. Pretty girl asks him into her apartment for a drink, he refuses. What d'you suppose he was afraid of?"

"I can't imagine," Hawes said. "You never saw any girls in his place, huh?"

"No. Who'd bother with a bricklayer? I think I'll have another." She poured another. "You want one?"

"No, thanks."

"You might as well make yourself comfortable," she said.

"I've got a lot of other people to question."

"That must be a drag," she answered. "Specially on Saturday night. Don't you drink?"

"I drink."

"So have one."

"Not now, thanks."

"Look, everybody else on this floor is out. This is Saturday night. This is the night everybody goes out to howl, you know? Saturday, you know? Don't you know what Saturday is?"

"Sure, I know," Hawes said.

"So don't you know how to howl?"

"Sure, I know how to howl."

"So have a drink. There ain't nobody on this floor left to question, anyway. 'Cept me. And I'm all alone. Just me, huh? You ask the questions. I got all the answers. Jenny Pelenco's got all the answers."

"Except the ones I want," Hawes said.

"Huh?"

"You don't know anything at all about Fetterick, huh?"

"I told you. A jerk. A bum. A bricklayer. A jerk. A guy who lays bricks."

"Well, thanks a lot," Hawes said, rising.

Jenny Pelenco drank her whiskey and then looked at Hawes steadily. "What do *you* lay?" she asked.

Hawes moved to the door. "Good night, Mrs. Pelenco," he said. "When you write to your husband, tell him the police department appreciated all the help you gave them. That should please him." He opened the door.

Jenny Pelenco did not take her eyes from him. "What do *you* lay, cop?" she asked.

"Carpets," Hawes said politely, and he walked out of the apartment.

As he walked down the steps, Jenny yelled after him, *"Carpets?"*

They walked on each side of the black coffin, the men who had worked with him. They walked in solemn regularity. The coffin seemed light, but only because its weight was evenly distributed upon the shoulders of the detectives.

They put the coffin into the hearse, and then the black cars followed the hearse out to Sands Spit and the cemetery. There were some of Havilland's relatives there, but not many. Havilland was a man who'd lived almost entirely alone. The priest said some words over the open grave, and then the coffin was lowered on its canvas strips, and the detectives bent their heads and watched their erstwhile colleague enter the ground. It was a beautiful June day. Havilland could not have asked for a nicer day.

The gravediggers began shoveling earth into the hole as the funeral party dispersed.

The cars drove away in the bright June sunshine, and the detectives got back to work. There were still two murders to be solved.

Roger Havilland lay in the ground, no longer a part of it. A stone would be erected over his grave within the next two weeks. Relatives might visit his grave with flowers annually, and then perhaps the relatives might stop their visits, the flowers would stop.

Roger Havilland would never know or care.

Roger Havilland was no longer a part of it.

Roger Havilland was dead and buried.

CHAPTER 11

IF THERE is anything worse than being interrogated by one cop, it is being interrogated by *two* cops. There is something unnerving about having to face two men who ask questions with blank faces. It is perhaps this psychological rattling which accounts for detectives working in pairs. The pair facing Patricia Colworthy was composed of Detective Meyer Meyer and Detective Bert Kling. She had never seen a blanker pair of faces in her life. When they first arrived, she'd honestly believed they were undertakers come to announce the death of her long-ailing aunt in Tucson. Instead, they'd turned out to be cops. They didn't look at all like Joe Friday or Frank Smith. They were very disappointing, to tell the truth. The blond one was sort of cute, but his face was as blank as the bald one's. Together, they looked like an advertisement for rivets.

"We got your name from Annie Boone's address book," the bald one said. "We assumed she was a friend of yours."

"Yes," Patricia Colworthy said.

"How close a friend, Miss Colworthy?" the blond one asked.

"Pretty close."

"How long have you known her?"

"Two years at least."

"Did you know she was divorced?" That from the blond one.

"Yes."

"Did you know her ex-husband?" That from the bald one.

"No."

"Ted Boone?"

"No."

"When did you see her last?"

"Two Saturdays ago. We double-dated."

"With whom?"

"Two fellers."

"Yes. Who were they?"

"My boy friend. Steve Brasil. And a boy Annie was with."

"His name?"

"Frank. Frank Abelson."

"Had you seen Abelson before that Saturday?"

"Yes. She dated with him every once in a while."

"Anything serious between them?"

"No, I don't think so. Why don't you question her ex-husband? From what Annie told me, he was trying to get the kid back. He had a *reason* for killing Annie. Abelson had no reason. He's a nice guy."

"Mr. Boone may have had a reason," the blond one said, "but not an opportunity. Mr. Boone was forty miles away from the city when his ex-wife was killed. A counter-man at a diner is ready to identify him. He couldn't have killed Annie."

"He's out, huh?"

"He's out."

"Well, Frank Abelson didn't do it, either. I'll bet he has a good alibi, too. You going to question him?"

"Maybe."

"Why don't you question the right people?"

"Like who?" the blond one asked.

"The right people."

"Was Annie Boone a drunkard?" the bald one asked.

"A what?"

"A drunkard."

"Are you kidding?"

"I'm serious."

"Where'd you hear *that?*"

"We heard."

"Boy, is *that* all wet. Boy, that takes the cake!"

"She *wasn't* a drunkard?"

"I think the strongest thing she ever drank was sherry. A drunkard! Boy, that's a lulu, all right."

"Are you sure?"

"Sure, I'm sure. I went out with her a lot. Maybe a glass

or two of sherry. Or maybe a cordial. Never whiskey. A drunkard! Wow!"

The bald one looked at the blond one.

"Somebody told you she was a drunkard?" Patricia asked.

"Yes."

"Well, you gotta be careful. There's people who are out to protect their own interests, you know. They don't care how they malign a dead person."

"Which people did you have in mind, Miss?" the bald one asked.

"People. People always got their own axes to grind, don't you know that?"

"Did you like Annie?"

"Loved her like a sister. I didn't like everything she was involved in, but that's none of my business. I like a person, I like them. I don't ask questions. I don't stick my nose where it don't belong."

"What sort of things?"

"Huh?"

"Was she involved in?"

"Oh. That's none of my business."

"But it *is* ours," the bald one said.

He wasn't so bad when you got used to him. He had nice blue eyes, and a very patient manner.

"Yeah, but . . . I don't like to talk about somebody's dead."

"Well, it might help us to find her murderer."

"That's true. Still. I wouldn't like nobody talking about me if I was dead." Patricia shivered. "Whooo! That gives me the creeps, you know? I got goose bumps all over me, just talking about it. I can't stand talking about death, do you know? I couldn't even go to my own mother's funeral, that's how bad I am. When you two first got here, I thought you were undertakers, and I got goose bumps all over. I got an aunt out West is ready to die any day now. I get the creeps thinking about it."

The blond one looked at the bald one.

"No offense meant," Patricia said. "About the undertakers, I mean. It's just you were so serious and all."

The bald one looked at the blond one.

"Well," Patricia said, and she gave up.

96

"What was Annie Boone involved in?" the blond one asked.

"Nothing."

"Something illegal?"

"No."

"Bootleg hootch?"

"Huh?"

"Tax evasion?"

"Huh?"

"What was it?"

"Nothing."

"*Not* something illegal?"

"No. I don't know. How do I know it's legal or not."

"What?"

"What she was doing."

"What was she doing?"

"I don't know. She was my friend. Look, I don't like to talk about somebody's dead. Can't we change the subject? Can't we talk about something else?"

"Was she a drunkard?" the bald one asked.

"No."

"A junkie?" the blond one asked.

"A what?"

"A drug addict?"

"No."

"What then? What was she doing illegally?"

"Nothing."

"Then why'd she get killed so violently?"

"I don't know. Why don't you ask . . ." Patricia stopped.

"Ask who?"

"Ask . . . other people."

"Like who?"

"Like the people she knew better than me. Like Frank Abelson. He knew her better. Or this other feller she dated. Artie Cordis. Ask them."

"Was she serious with them?"

"No."

"Then why should we ask them anything?"

"I don't know. It's better than asking me. I don't know about her, or about what she was doing."

"Who'd want to kill her, Miss Colworthy?"

"How should I know? I don't even like to talk about it. I don't even like to *think* about it!"

97

"Did she have any enemies?"

"No."

"Close friends?"

Patricia did not answer.

"Who?"

Patricia did not answer.

"All right," the bald one said, sighing. "Who was she sleeping with?"

Patricia sighed, too.

"Mr. Phelps," she said. "The man who owned the liquor shop where she worked."

Franklin Phelps did not live in the 87th Precinct.

His liquor store was there, but he lived in a fashionable suburb called Northern Crestion. He lived in a house which had cost him $35,000 ten years ago, and which he could have listed now with any real estate agent for $49,500. The house itself wasn't anything to go shouting about. But it happened that Northern Crestion had sort of grown up around the house, and real estate values had grown with it.

The house was on a half acre of ground, set back some fifty feet from the road. The road itself was called Pala Vista Drive, and Meyer and Kling drove up the winding street looking at the numbers on the stone pillars of each driveway. They stopped at number 35 Pala Vista. They left the car at the curb, and then walked up the wide slate pathway to the front door. The house was a two-story frame with hand-split cedar shingles and shutters. The shingles had been painted a teal blue. The shutters were white. The door was white, too, and there was a big brass knocker in the center of it. Meyer lifted the knocker and let it fall.

"Ten-to-one a servant," he said to Kling.

"No bet," Kling answered.

The door opened. A colored girl in a pink uniform peered out at them.

"Yes?" she asked.

"Mr. Phelps, please."

"Who shall I say is calling, please?"

"Police," Meyer said, and he flashed the tin.

"Just a moment, please," the girl said, and she closed the door gently.

"Think he'll make a run through the back door?" Meyer asked jokingly.

98

"Maybe so," Kling answered. "Shall I get the riot gun from the car?"

"Some hand grenades, too," Meyer said. "It's too bad Mr. Cotton isn't with us. I haven't been shot in a long time."

The door opened again. An attractive woman of forty-two, perhaps closer to forty-four, stood in the doorway. Her hair had once been blond, but it was turning grey, turning with a gentle dignity. She had large brown eyes, and she smiled pleasantly and said, "Won't you come in? Franklin's in the shower."

The detectives stepped into the foyer. A smoky grey mirror threw their reflections back at them.

"Won't you come into the living room?" she said. "I'm Marna Phelps."

"I'm Detective Meyer," Meyer said. "My partner, Detective Kling."

"How do you do?" Mrs. Phelps said. "Would you like some coffee or anything? Franklin won't be but a moment."

They followed her into the living room. The furniture was straight from the palace at Versailles. A Louis XVI writing cabinet with a fall-down front stood against the wall between two windows, three circular and three rectangular Sèvres porcelain plaques set into its face. A Regency mahogany library table was against the opposite wall, flanked by a pair of Louis XVI giltwood settees, their seats and backs upholstered in Beauvais tapestry. Rare porcelain and china were spotted indiscreetly about the room. Meyer expected Marie Antoinette to come in serving tea and cakes. Uneasily, the detectives sat.

"Did you say you wanted coffee?" Mrs. Phelps asked.

"No, thank you," Kling said.

Meyer cleared his throat and looked at Kling. He would, in fact, have enjoyed a cup of coffee. The opportunity was past. Mrs. Phelps was turning to a new topic.

"This is about Annie, isn't it?" she asked.

"Yes," Kling said.

"You know then?"

"Know what?"

"About Franklin and her?"

"What did you mean, Mrs. Phelps?" Meyer asked.

"That they were having an affair?" Mrs. Phelps said.

Kling blinked. Meyer, being a slightly older man, did not blink.

"Yes, we know," he said.

"He didn't kill her," Mrs. Phelps said. "I can assure you."

"How long have you known about this?"

"The affair? For a long time."

"How long?"

"At least a year." Mrs. Phelps shrugged. "Franklin isn't exactly a spring chicken. I wasn't worried. These things happen, I understand. If I'd made a fuss about it, I might have lost him. I have too much invested in him to see it all go down the drain. Under ordinary circumstances, the thing would have been over in another six months, anyway. Unfortunately, Miss Boone was killed."

"Did you know her, Mrs. Phelps?"

"I met her on one or two occasions, yes. At the store."

"What did you think of her?"

"A very beautiful girl. Franklin's taste is to be admired."

"Your attitude is a pretty broad-minded one, isn't it, Mrs. Phelps?"

"Are you married, Detective . . . Meyer, was it?"

"Yes."

"Ask your wife. Ask her about the time she's put into shaping you into a man. It's an investment, Detective Meyer. A simple investment. A woman's man is her only investment. And her children, of course, if she's lucky enough to have them. I have no children. Do you have children, Detective Meyer?"

"Yes. Three."

"Your wife is luckier than I. I only have Franklin. He is my sole investment, my life work; men have other things, women only have their men. He is my business. And I have thrown assets into this business, Detective Meyer. I have given Franklin everything I had to give. Everything. I've been a good wife. And as a result, he's a man today. He was not very much of a man when we met. I saw potential. I invested. The only thing I had to invest: *myself.*"

"I see," Meyer said.

"And so, when my investment is threatened by a beautiful woman, I do what my common sense tells me to do. I sit, and I wait. I'm not going to close shop because of a small fire in the stockroom, am I?" Mrs. Phelps smiled pleasantly. "It would have been over in another six months. Things would have gone on again."

"Did Annie Boone know you knew?"

"No."

"Did your husband?"

"No. He still doesn't. I wish you wouldn't tell him. It's not good for a wife to appear too intelligent." Again, Mrs. Phelps smiled. "But then, I'm giving you trade secrets, Detective Meyer. I'll be spoiling things for your wife."

"She doesn't need hints," Meyer said, smiling. "She's got her own investment."

"Are you going to confront him with what you know?"

"Yes."

"I wish you wouldn't. I don't think it'll help much. He's not the person who killed her."

"Who *is?*" Meyer asked.

"I'm sure I don't know," Mrs. Phelps said. She smiled. "May I sound somewhat cruel for a moment?"

"Go ahead," Meyer said.

Mrs. Phelps was still smiling. "I'm sure I don't *give* a damn, either," she said.

"Don't give a damn about what, dear?" Franklin Phelps asked from the doorway.

"Don't give a damn about showing our dogs," she answered, adjusting her mind almost instantly to the new situation.

"Oh," Phelps said. He smiled at the detectives. "We've got a trio of Goldens. I want to show them, Marna doesn't. Handsome animals." He looked at Meyer. "Oh, Detective Meyer. I didn't recognize you."

"Hello, Mr. Phelps," Meyer said, rising and taking his hand. "This is my partner, Bert Kling."

"Detective Kling," Phelps said, and he took his hand. He was a tall man with greying hair, and he wore a blue terry cloth robe belted at the waist. He had not impressed Meyer very much the first time Meyer had questioned him, but a man is always looked at somewhat differently when it's learned he was having an affair with a beautiful red-head perhaps ten years younger than he. Phelps had a strong sweeping nose, and piercing grey eyes. His mouth was full and hard. His jaw could have driven railroad spikes.

"I'm sorry we got you out of the shower, Mr. Phelps,"

Meyer said, "but we'd like to ask you a few more questions."

"I behaved like a bit of an ass last time we spoke, didn't I?" Phelps said.

"Well," Meyer answered noncommittally.

"I really shouldn't have carried on so about my stock. I really shouldn't have."

"Well, there was a lot of money involved," Meyer said.

"Certainly, but after checking with my broker, I found out my insurance covered the loss."

"Oh," Meyer said flatly. "I see."

"I'm glad to clear the air on that," Phelps said. "I didn't want you to have the impression I was an ass."

"Well, I never got that impression," Meyer lied. "Could we talk to you, Mr. Phelps?"

"Certainly, go right ahead," Phelps said smiling. He went to a small Louis XVI table, removed the cover from a porcelain box, and picked up a cigarette. He was lighting it when Meyer said, "Alone."

The match faltered for just an instant. Phelps brought it to the cigarette again and said, "Certainly. Marna?"

"I've got a million things to do, anyway," Mrs. Phelps said. "It was nice meeting you gentlemen." She smiled again and left the room.

"What is it?" Phelps asked.

"We'd like to run over the information you already gave us, Mr. Phelps," Meyer said.

"Certainly." He puffed on his cigarette, one hand in the pocket of his robe.

"How long did you say you'd known Annie Boone?"

"She'd been working for me about a year," Phelps said.

"Yes. How long before that had you known her?"

"I met her for the first time when she answered an ad I placed in the newspaper."

"What was your relationship with Annie Boone?"

"I was her employer."

"How much did you pay her?"

"A hundred and twenty-five dollars a week."

"Do you remember sending her roses once when she was ill?" Kling asked.

"I don't recall."

"You did," Kling said.

"Perhaps."

"Isn't that a little unusual?"

"If I did send them, I don't see anything unusual about it. Annie was a trusted employee. Without her, I could not have run that shop."

"When did you first meet, Mr. Phelps?"

"When she answered my ad."

"Where did you run the ad?"

"In most of the local dailies."

"Why did you hire her?"

"She'd had selling experience."

"Selling whiskey?"

"No. Furniture."

"Where had she sold furniture?"

"Herman Dodson, Inc.," Phelps said.

"She told you that?"

"Yes."

"You remember it?"

"Yes, certainly."

"Was Annie a drunkard?"

"A what?"

"A drunkard."

"That's preposterous! Of course not!"

"How do you know?"

"Well, I never saw her drink more than a glass of . . ." Phelps paused.

"A glass of what, Mr. Phelps?"

"Wine," he completed.

"Where was this, Mr. Phelps?"

"I don't remember."

"You knew her socially, did you, Mr. Phelps?"

"Socially? No, no, of course not. I don't remember where I saw her drink. Perhaps at the store."

"Your stock?"

"Yes. Yes, my stock."

"What was the occasion?"

"No occasion. We . . . we opened a bottle of wine."

"Was that the only time you saw her drink?"

"Yes."

"Then how do you know she wasn't a drunkard?"

"Well, a man can tell, can't he? She worked for me, you know. I saw her in the shop, and she was never drunk."

"How much did you pay her, Mr. Phelps?"

"I told you. A hundred and twenty-five dollars a week.

What is this? A third degree of some kind? Am I going to have to call my lawyer?"

"You can if you wish, Mr. Phelps. You can very easily do that. I suggest, however, that you sit tight and start answering some of these questions straight."

"I'm answering as honestly as I know how. I don't have to answer a damn thing if I don't want to."

"You will if we book you."

"On what charge?"

"Suspicion of murder," Kling said flatly.

Phelps was silent for a moment.

"I think I'd better call my lawyer," he said at last.

"If that's what you plan, Mr. Phelps," Meyer said, "you'll have to call him after we get to the squad room."

Phelps blinked.

"Here or there," Meyer said. "You can answer the questions anywhere you like. If you didn't kill her, you've got nothing to fear."

"I didn't kill her."

"Okay. Why'd you lie to us then?"

"I haven't lied to you."

"Were you having an affair with Annie Boone?"

Phelps was silent.

"Were you?"

"Yes," he said.

"Why didn't you tell us that in the beginning?"

"For several reasons."

"Like?"

"First, I didn't want to get involved in a possible murder charge."

"That possibility still exists, Mr. Phelps."

"Secondly, I thought this might make the newspapers. I didn't want Marna to . . . well, you understand."

"Sure," Meyer said. "Now how about giving us the straight story?"

"Where do you want me to start?"

"Where'd you meet Annie?"

Phelps sighed heavily. "At Herman Dodson, Inc. In the modern furniture department. I wandered onto the wrong floor by mistake. Marna and I prefer period stuff."

"Go ahead."

"I asked her out. She accepted. Oh, not quite that suddenly. We chatted awhile, you know how it works."

"No, I don't know how it works," Meyer said. "I'm married. You tell me how it works, Mr. Phelps."

"I didn't know policemen were invested with moral indignation," Phelps said. "I didn't know love was a crime in this state."

"It isn't," Meyer said. "But adultery *is*."

"Annie wasn't married!" Phelps said.

"You were, and are. The law makes it adultery if either or both partners are married. Let's not get off the track, Mr. Phelps. The crime we're discussing is homicide!"

"I didn't kill her."

"We're still listening."

"I loved her. Why should I kill her?"

"You didn't seem to be worrying too damn much about her the first time I spoke to you. You seemed more concerned with your stock."

"I was concerned with the stock. But I was concerned about Annie, too. Of course I was concerned. I'd known her for more than a year."

"Why'd you give her a job at the liquor store? So you could be closer to her?"

"Well . . . not exactly. I very rarely went to the shop. Annie handled it mostly singlehanded. I dropped by at the end of the day, usually, to make my collection."

"Had you dropped by on the night she was killed?"

"Yes. I told you that before. I'd left her just enough money to keep things going until closing time. That was the usual procedure. I made out my bank deposit slips every night and made my deposit each morning."

"Which bank?"

"Here. In town. First National of Crestion."

"Why'd you give her the job?"

"To help her."

"How?"

"She was divorced, you know. She wasn't earning a hell of a lot at Dodson. I found that out after I'd . . . after I'd known her awhile. I thought I could help her by taking her on. I paid her more than a hundred and a quarter."

"How much more?"

"I paid her two hundred dollars a week," Phelps said.

"Did Mrs. Phelps know this?"

"No, of course not. The highest I'd ever paid any employee was a hundred and a quarter."

"In other words, Mr. Phelps," Meyer said, "you charged Annie Boone to the business, is that right?"

"That's a particularly callous way to put it, Detective Meyer."

"Is it? How would you put it, Mr. Phelps?"

"I was trying to help the girl. She was supporting her mother and her daughter. It was the least I could do."

"Sure. Why'd you pretend you didn't know about the daughter when I first talked to you, Mr. Phelps?"

"I pretended no such thing."

"You said you thought she had a son."

"Well, perhaps I did. I lied because I didn't want the police to know how involved I was with Annie. I didn't want her murder to . . . to reflect upon me."

"What time did you make your collection on the night she was killed, Mr. Phelps?"

"At about eight. I always make my collection at about that time."

"She was killed at about ten-thirty, near as we can figure it. Where were you between eight and ten-thirty?"

"I don't remember," Phelps said quickly.

Meyer looked at him with something close to vast astonishment on his face. "Mr. Phelps," he said, "perhaps you didn't understand my question. Where were you on the night Annie Boone was killed between the hours of eight and ten-thirty?"

"I don't remember," Phelps said.

Meyer continued to look astonished. "Well, maybe you better start remembering, Mr. Phelps. Maybe you better start remembering damn fast."

"If I don't remember, I don't remember."

"Were you here?" Kling asked.

"No, I wasn't."

"Where then?"

"I don't remember."

"But you do remember that you weren't here?"

"Yes, I remember that."

"Were you maybe in your own liquor store shooting Annie Boone and destroying your own stock maybe?" Meyer asked.

"Don't be ridiculous!"

"Well then, where the hell were you, Mr. Phelps? Start

106

remembering. I suggest that you start remembering!"

"Look . . ."

"Look *what?*"

"Look, I don't want you to think . . ." Phelps shook his head. "Look, I . . ."

"Go ahead, Mr. Phelps. Drag out the skeletons."

"Did you question Ted Boone? Did you question her ex-husband?"

"He was out of the city at the time of the shooting. His alibi has been corroborated. He's clear, Mr Phelps."

"So am I."

"We haven't heard *your* alibi yet."

"I don't remember where I was. I was nowhere near the store."

Meyer sighed heavily. "Mr. Phelps," he said. "Get your clothes on."

"Why?"

"Because it looks as if you haven't got a story, Mr. Phelps. It also looks as if you were pretty involved with this Boone girl, and it looks as if we've got to ask you a few more questions at the squad. A *lot* more questions, Mr. Phelps."

"I . . ." Phelps swallowed hard. "I . . . I was in Isola that night."

"Where in Isola?"

"On . . . Endicott Avenue."

"Doing what?"

"I . . . I was with someone."

"Who?" Phelps did not answer. "Who?" Meyer repeated.

"Someone."

"Who?" Kling said.

"A woman?" Meyer asked.

"Yes," Phelps said.

Both detectives were silent. At last Meyer said, "You're a real nice chap, Mr. Phelps. You're a real fine invest-ment."

"Investment?"

"The ones who own stock in you ought to liquidate it. What's the broad's name?"

"She's not a broad!"

"What's her name?"

"Lydia. Lydia Forrester."

"Address?"

"730 Endicott Avenue. You're not going to drag her into this, are you?"

"Can you think of a better way of checking your alibi?"

"I suppose not."

"Any doormen at her place? Elevator operators?"

"Yes, why?"

"Mr. Phelps, the way this thing looks to be shaping up, you've now got a pretty damn good reason for wanting Annie Boone out of the way. And I don't know if we're going to be happy with just the Reason's word that you were with her that night. You better keep your fingers crossed."

"About what?"

"You better keep your fingers crossed that somebody else in that building saw you around the time Annie was murdered." Meyer nodded emphatically. "We'll see you, Mr. Phelps. We'll let you know. You can be sure we'll let you know."

CHAPTER 12

IT'S VERY discouraging to learn that a man suspected of murder has an airtight alibi. It was discouraging to learn it about Ted Boone and even more discouraging to learn it about Franklin Phelps. But the sad facts remained. Franklin Phelps had been with a girl named Lydia Forrester from 9 P.M. until 11 P.M. on the night Annie Boone got it. The elevator operator remembered taking him up at 9 and down at 11. This did not mean, of course, that he could not have taken the service steps down at any time between those two times, gone out to kill Annie, and then come back up again by the same steps. The service steps, however, terminated in one of two places: the lobby, or the basement. A doorman was on duty in the lobby all night long. Franklin Phelps had not crossed it until 11 P.M. And the superintendent and the janitor had been playing cards in the basement all night long, right alongside the only exit door. Phelps had not come down to the basement. Phelps had been otherwise occupied. He had not killed Annie Boone, and it was most discouraging. It meant that the bulls of the 87th had to do more legwork, and it's the legwork that kills a cop.

For reasons which weren't even clear to themselves, it seemed as if every cop on the squad was taking turns at the legwork involved in finding the murderer of Annie Boone. Every cop but Cotton Hawes. Cotton Hawes had his own private little crusade going against the man who'd murdered Roger Havilland. It made things cozy, though, everyone being involved. It gave them all a sort of personal stake. It also gave them something to talk about when they didn't have any dirty jokes to tell. It was nice. It was brotherly.

"This legwork is a son of a bitch," Carella said to Kling. "When you get to be my age, anyway. Of course, with a kid like you, it doesn't matter. How old are you, anyway, Bert? Seventeen?"

"*Six*teen," Kling said.

"Sure. These steps don't matter to you."

"I eat steps," Kling said.

"Sure."

"I eat sidewalks."

"Sure."

They were climbing the steps to a pool parlor known euphemistically as "Heaven's Hall." The steps leading upstairs did not at all smell like heaven. Kling didn't know what they smelled like, but they certainly didn't smell like heaven.

"When I was a boy," Carella said, "I used to eat steps, too. Sidewalks, too."

"No more now," Kling said. "You're up for pension, aren't you?"

"Sure."

"How old are you anyway, Steve?" Kling asked. "Sixty-eight?"

"Sixty-*nine*," Carella said.

"Sure. You look pretty good, though, I have to admit it. You don't look too bad at all."

"Clean living," Carella said.

They had reached Heaven's Hall. They could hear the inimitable sound of pool balls being knocked around on green felt. Together they walked to the small booth at the entrance to the place. The booth was really an L-shaped glass-fronted cigar stand. A bald-headed man and a light panel for the tables were behind the stand. The bald-headed man didn't even look up when they approached. He had the drawer of the cash register open, and he was counting money.

When he finished, Carella asked, "Good day?"

"*Comme ci, comme ça,*" the bald-headed man said. "If you want a table, you got to wait. I'm all full up." He shifted his cigar butt to the other side of his mouth.

"We don't want a table," Carella said.

"No? So what do you want?"

"A man named Frank Abelson."

"What for?"

110

"Police," Carella said. He flashed the tin.

"What'd he do?"

"Just want to ask him a few questions," Carella said.

"What about?"

"Routine."

"What kind of routine?"

"Routine routine," Carella said.

"It ain't about . . ."

"About what?"

"Nothing." The bald-headed man looked worried.

"What's the matter?"

"Nothing. My name's Fink. Baldy Fink. That's a funny name, ain't it?"

"Yeah," Carella said.

"Ring a bell?"

"What?"

"The name. Baldy Fink. Ring a bell?"

"No. Should it?"

"This ain't about the . . . uh . . . it ain't, huh?"

"The what?" Carella asked.

"Baldy Fink don't ring a bell, huh?"

"No."

"You know this guy at the 87th? You from the 87th?"

"Yeah."

"Havilland? Roger Havilland? He's a bull. You know him?"

Kling looked at Carella. "Yeah, we know him."

"Well . . . uh . . . how much do you guys tell each other? I mean, what kind of arrangements do you have going?"

"I don't understand," Carella said.

"I mean . . . do you split, or what?"

"Split what?"

"The take."

"What take?"

"Come on, you ain't that young a cop," Fink said.

"You were paying Havilland?" Carella asked.

"Sure."

"What for?"

"The crap games."

"You run crap games here, do you?"

"Sure. It's okay. Havilland said it was okay. He said no cops would bother me."

"Havilland's dead," Kling said.

Fink opened his mouth. "Yeah?"

"Yeah."

"Oh, I see. You come to take over, huh?" Fink shrugged. "Okay, suits me. I don't care who gets it, long as I'm left alone. Same deal as with him?"

"Not exactly," Carella said.

"More?"

"Not exactly."

"What then?"

"No more crap games," Carella said.

"Huh?"

"No more crap games."

"Why the hell not?"

"New administration," Carella said.

"Ah, come on. Hey, that ain't nice. I mean, you sucked me right into this."

"You did all the talking, Fink," Carella said. "We only listened."

"Sure, so what kind of a way is that to act? Don't you want what Havilland was getting?"

"No."

"Come on."

"No," Carella said. "Call off the crap games. Find another sewer."

"Argh, shat, you guys," Fink said disgustedly.

"Where's Abelson?"

"Table number three. He don't like to be disturbed when he's shootin' pool."

"That's too bad," Carella said, and he and Kling walked over to table number three. There was only one man shooting at the table. He wore a white shirt and a blue weskit open over the shirt. His sleeves were rolled up. He had dark hair with a pronounced widow's peak, and sharp brown eyes. Even though he was alone at the table, he called off all his shots aloud.

"Six in the corner," he said. He shot, and the cue ball hit the six. The six went straight for the corner pocket and the cue stopped on a dime behind the thirteen ball.

"Thirteen in the side," Abelson said.

"Frank Abelson?" Kling asked.

"Yeah. Quiet a minute. Thirteen in the side." He shot and sank the thirteen ball. The cue ball hit the cushion, ricocheted, and rolled over to the eight ball.

112

"Eight in the . . ."

"Hold your game a minute, Abelson," Kling said.

Abelson looked up. "Who says?"

"Police," Kling answered.

Abelson walked to one end of the table. He picked up the chalk and began chalking the end of his stick. "I was wondering when you'd get around to me," he said. "I can listen while I play."

He stepped behind the cue ball, ducked below the table so that his eyes were level with the rim. "Eight in the far corner," he said. He took his position and triggered off the cue. The eight shot for the far corner in a straight line.

"Why'd you figure we'd get around to you?"

"This is about Annie, isn't it?"

"Yes."

"So? It figures. I took her out. So here you are. What do you want to know?"

"You can start by telling us where you were on the night she was killed."

"What night was that?" Abelson asked. "Eleven in the corner." He shot.

"The night of June 10th."

"What night was that? I mean like Monday, Tuesday, you know."

"Monday."

"Jeez, that's a hard night to figure. Four in the side." He shot, and then chalked his stick again. "Who the hell remembers?"

"It was a week ago yesterday," Kling reminded him.

"A week ago yesterday. Lemme see. Five in the same pocket." He studied the shot. "No, make it in the corner. No, leave it in the side."

"A buck you don't make it," Carella said.

"I don't take candy from babies," Abelson said. He shot. The five ball disappeared into the side pocket. "See?"

"You play here a lot?"

"A little."

"You're pretty good."

"I'm okay." Abelson studied the table. "Bank the deuce into this side," he said.

"What about the night of June 10th?"

"I'm thinking," Abelson said. He shot and missed the

113

pocket by a hair. "Damnit," he said. "You're throwing off my game."

"That's a real shame," Kling said. "Tell us about the 10th."

"I was busy."

"Doing what?"

"Yeah, I remember now."

"What were you doing?"

"What the hell difference does it make? I was nowhere near that liquor shop."

"What were you doing?"

Abelson lowered his voice. "You guys in on the fix?"

"The Havilland deal?"

"Yeah."

"No."

"Oh. Oh," Abelson said.

"Was there a crap game here that Monday night?"

"Well . . ."

"We know about the fix. It's okay," Kling said.

"Well, yeah, there was a sort of a game. I cleaned up, kind of."

"How much?"

"Five bills. That's okay, ain't it? I mean for a small-time game."

"Yeah, pretty good. Don't forget to declare it."

"Oh, I won't. Honest, that's me. Legal."

"What time'd you get here?"

"About eight."

"And you left?"

"Around two in the morning."

"You were here all that time?"

"Sure. I was hot."

"I suppose you were seen here all that time."

"Sure."

"Fink see you?"

"Sure. Him and a lot of other guys."

"How well did you know Annie?"

"Pretty well. Dated her on and off." Abelson blinked. "Ain't you gonna check my alibi?"

"We'll get to it. How well is pretty well?"

"You know. Pretty well."

"Did you ever plank her?"

"Hey, what the hell kind of a question is that?"

114

"We'd like to know," Carella said.

"Why?"

"We'd like to know. You care to tell us?"

"Yeah, I did." He shook his head. "Boy, you guys don't believe in nothing private, do you? Nothing sacred."

"Did you know she was being kept by somebody?"

"Who? Who, Annie? You kidding?"

"We're serious."

"No, I didn't know that. I kinda liked her. She was a nice doll."

"Where'd you meet?"

"Shootin' pool, how d'you like that? She shoots pool. What a crazy doll, she was. Pep, you know. She come in this pool hall, not this one, another one called Mickey's. You know Mickey's? Well, she come in there one night, wearin' this dress cut to here, I swear it. She gets herself a table, racks them up, and starts sinkin' them like she's been workin' the tables all her life. What a crazy doll! Everytime she leaned over that table to make a shot, every eye in the place popped out. What a doll! I kinda liked her."

"She never told you about a man named Phelps?"

"No."

"You knew she was divorced?"

"Oh, sure. I used to go for her at the house, you know? I even met the kid. Monica. A nice little kid. I used to bring the kid things sometimes. Candy. A doll, once. Like that. She was a crazy little kid, that kid. Crazy. I mean, like gone. Not nuts."

"Sure."

"I kinda liked her, too."

"Ever think of marrying Annie?"

"I didn't like her *that* much, mister," Abelson said.

"She ever mention any enemies to you?"

"Nope."

"Anyone she was afraid of?"

"Nope."

"When did you see her last?"

"Well, I went over to the funeral parlor, to pay my respects."

"Alive, I mean."

"A few weeks ago. Wait, it was the first of the month. June 1st, I remember. Somebody made some comment about it being June already. June 1st. It was a Saturday night."

"Did she mention anything about a letter she'd received?"

"No."

"Did you call her after that night?"

"Yeah, I spoke to her a couple of times."

"Did she mention a letter during those conversations?"

"Not that I remember."

"Did you call her any time after June 6th?" Kling asked.

"Yeah, maybe. I think so."

"Mention a letter?"

"No."

"Did you know a man named Arthur Cordis?"

"Nope."

"A man named Jamie?"

"Nope. Well, wait. Jamie what?"

"We don't know his last name."

"No. I know some Jimmys, but they don't call themselves Jamies. Besides, they're nobody Annie knew. No, I'm sorry. You gonna check my alibi?"

"Yeah," Carella said. "She didn't seem worried about anything when you saw her? Nobody'd been bothering her, or threatening her, or anything?"

"She didn't say nothing about it. She seemed pretty happy. We had a ball. She was a real crazy doll. You shoulda seen her shoot pool, I mean it. She shot pool better than any guy I know. Except me. She was a real good pool player. Crazy. Crazy."

"You don't have any idea who might have done this to her, huh, Abelson?"

"None. She was a crazy doll. Who'd wanta kill her? It's a shame. It's really a goddamn shame. I kinda liked her, you know? I really kinda liked her a lot."

"Well, thanks a lot, Abelson," the detectives said, and they walked over to where Baldy Fink was recounting his money.

"Was Abelson at the crap game last Monday night?" Kling asked.

"Yeah," Fink said.

"From what time to what time?"

116

"Got here about eight-thirty, left sometime in the morning."

"What time?"

"Two, three. Somewhere around there."

"Did he leave at all during that time?"

"Leave? He was hot as a pistol. He won close to half a grand. When you asked about him, that's what I thought it was about. The crap game. He was here all night. That's what I thought it was about. Listen, can't you guys change your mind?"

"Anybody else see him here all night?"

"A hundred guys."

"Who?"

"Some of those guys right there," Fink said. "Table four."

Kling walked over to the table and began talking to the players.

"Can't we fix this up?" Fink asked. "What the hell, are you so honest?"

"It's not that I'm honest," Carella said. "I don't want to destroy your faith. I'm as crooked as every other cop you ever met. It's just that I've got bigger things going for me. I can't be bothered with small potatoes."

"Oh," Fink said, satisfied. "Oh, I see. Well, that explains it. I thought there was something fishy, you know? A cop who wouldn't take. I figured there was something. Listen, why don't you send around a bull who maybe ain't got such big things going for him, huh? I mean, like this'll be a big pain in the ass to change the game someplace else, you know?"

"Sure. And also you wouldn't get the house cut."

"Certainly. You understand. I got a big overhead here. A very big overhead. Find me a small potatoes cop, huh?"

"I'll look around," Carella said. "In the meantime, no game."

"Thanks," Fink said, pleased. "Thanks a million."

Kling came back to the booth.

"It checks out," he said. "Abelson's clean."

CHAPTER 13

THE KILLER of Annie Boone must have been getting worried.

The killer had no reason to worry because the police were nowhere near yet. But the killer remembered something and anticipated the police, and made a phone call—and perhaps that was a mistake.

The killer called the child.

The killer called Monica.

The killer asked her not to tell her grandmother she had spoken to anyone, but she told her grandmother anyway, and that was why she got a visit from Carella and Kling.

She recognized Kling the moment he came into the room.

She said, "Hi, ja find her?"

"Not yet," Kling said. He assumed the child still didn't know about her mother. Or if she did, she had adjusted to it miraculously well. "This is Detective Carella, Monica," Kling said.

"How do you do?" Monica asked.

"I hope this won't be a grueling experience for her," Mrs. Travail said. "She's only a child."

"We only want to ask a few questions, Mrs. Travail," Kling said. "This is Detective Carella."

"Yes," Mrs. Travail said, nodding briefly at Carella. "May I stay?"

"Certainly," Carella said, and he smiled at Mrs. Travail, and Kling noticed that she responded warmly to his smile, and he wondered what it was about Carella that made women respond warmly to his smile. He consoled himself with the knowledge that he still had Monica.

"You say the child received a phone call this morning, is that right?" Kling asked.

"Yes," Mrs. Travail answered. "So she says."

"Well, I did," Monica answered.

"I don't question it," Mrs. Travail said. She turned to the detectives. "It's just that she seems rather vague about it."

"What does vague mean?" Monica asked.

"*Did* you receive a phone call?" Kling asked, smiling.

"Sure, I did."

"What time was this?"

"I don't know."

"She can't tell time," Mrs. Travail said. "It was this morning sometime. I kept her home from school because she has the sniffles. Besides . . . I'm not too sure I trust her f-a-t-h-e-r."

"Father," Monica said, reading the spelling.

"After what happened, he may try to seize her. I'm not too keen on letting her out of the house."

"Do you think whoever called knew she was home?"

"I'm sure I don't know," Mrs. Travail said.

"Did this person who called ask for you, honey?" Kling asked.

"Yep. The person said, 'Is this Monica Boone?' and I said Yes, this is Monica Boone. That's how we started the conversation."

"Where was your grandmother?" Carella asked.

"I was down doing some shopping," Mrs. Travail answered.

"This person who called," Kling said. "Was it a man or a woman?"

"I don't know," Monica said.

"Didn't you talk to the person?"

"Yes."

"Well, was it a man or a woman?"

"I don't know."

"This is what I meant about her being vague," Mrs. Travail said.

"What does vague mean?" Monica asked again.

"It means you're not sure, honey," Kling said.

"Well, I'm not sure," Monica said, nodding.

"Had you ever heard this person's voice before?"

"No."

"This was the first time?"

"Yes."

"What kind of a voice was it?"

"I don't know."

"Well, you said you couldn't tell if it was a man or a woman. Was it a deep voice?"

"Sort of."

"Like a man's?"

"Sort of."

"But you're not sure?"

"No. It could have been a lady, too. It was hard to tell. It sounded as if the voice was coming . . . I don't know . . . through a long box or something. It was funny,"

"Through a handkerchief?" King asked Carella.

"Possibly. What did this person say to you, Monica?"

"Well, let me see. First it said, 'Is this Monica Boone?' and I said Yes, this is Monica Boone. Then it said, 'How are you, Monica?' and I said I'm fine, thank you, how are you? Grandmother told me to always be polite on the phone."

"Then what?"

"Then it said . . ."

"This person?"

"Yes. I don't know whether to say him or her."

"You can say 'it,' " Kling said.

"Well, it said, 'Would you like to be a good little girl?' So naturally I said Yes I'd like to be a good little girl. Then it said, 'Are you a smart little girl?' I don't like to boast, but I said I was a smart little girl."

"Then what?"

"Then it said, 'Your mother got a letter a week or so ago. In a blue envelope. Did you see it around the house any place?' Well, I couldn't remember seeing it, but I said, Maybe, who's this?"

"And what did the person say?"

"The person said, 'It doesn't matter who this is, Monica. This is a friend of Mommy's.' So I said Who?"

"Did the person tell you?"

"No. It just said, 'A friend of Mommy's. Did you see the letter?' I remember then that I did see the letter because Mommy was pretty upset when she got it. I mean, I remembered her opening it, and then looking pretty worried. You know how mothers are. They get worried over letters and things."

"Sure," Kling said. "Did you tell this person you'd seen the letter?"

"Yes."

"What did the person say?"

Sitting on the couch, Carella began to take notes on the telephone conversation. He used two names: Monica and Suspect. He did not bother to write down Kling's questions. He concentrated only on the telephone conversation between Monica and the suspect. He listened to every word, and he wrote every word down in his rapid longhand.

SUSPECT: Where did you see the letter, Monica?

MONICA: I don't know. When Mommy got it.

SUSPECT: She mentioned it to you?

MON: No. I saw her reading it.

SUS: She didn't tell you what was in it?

MON: No, she never tells me what's in her letters.

S: Was this letter in a blue envelope?

M: Yes.

S: Are you sure, Monica?

M: Yes. I remember because I said to Mommy, that's a pretty blue.

S: What did Mommy say?

M: She didn't say anything. She was bothered by the letter. You could tell she was bothered.

S: Did she say who it was from?

M: No.

S: Did she guess at it?

M: What do you mean?

S: Did she say anything about it being funny the letter wasn't signed?

M: No.

S: But did she seem to know who it was from?

M: No. Who is this, anyway?

S: A friend of Mommy's. Now think, Monica. What did Mommy do with the letter when she finished reading it?

M: I don't remember.

S: Think!

M: I am thinking. I don't remember. I have to go dress my dolly now.

S: Wait, Monica! Did she put it in her purse?

M: No. She didn't have her purse with her.

S: Where *did* she put it?

M: I don't know. She went to make a telephone call, I think.

S: Who'd she call?

M: I don't know.

S: The police?

M: I don't know. I know a cop, did you know that? He's a detective and he has a gun and everything.

S: Did you tell this detective about the letter?

M: No. Why should he care about an old letter? He was looking for a little girl who's missing.

S: Did you mention the letter to anyone?

M: No. Who cares about an old letter?

S: Now think, Monica.

M: I'm thinking. What is it?

S: Where's the letter now?

M: I don't know.

S: Is it still in the house?

M: I think so.

S: How do you know?

M: I saw it around some place, I think.

S: Where?

M: Some place.

S: But where, Monica?

M: I don't remember. I really have to go now. Dolly's lying all naked and everything.

S: Monica, think a minute.

M: Well, what is it because I really have to go. I don't want her to catch cold.

S: She won't catch cold. Where's the letter?

M: I already told you. I don't know. It's some place. Do you have any dolls?

S: No. Think, Monica.

M: For Pete's sake, I am thinking, you know. I'm thinking as hard as I can think. But my dolly . . .

S: Was it in the living room?

M: I don't remember.

S: The dining room?

M: We haven't got a dining room.

S: Mommy's bedroom?

M: Maybe. Maybe she put it in her desk.

S: Did she?

M: For Pete's sake, how do I know? You sure ask a lot of questions.

S: I'm only trying to help Mommy. That letter is very important. *Did* she put it in her desk?

M: Maybe.

S: Her closet, maybe?

M: Maybe.

S: Would you look?

M: Right now, you mean?

S: Yes.

M: Where do you want me to look?

S: In her desk, and in her closet.

M: Right now, you mean?

S: Yes.

M: I don't want to. Not right now. I have to dress Dolly.

S: When can you look?

M: I don't want to look. I'm not allowed in Mommy's drawers and things. She doesn't allow it. She says it's invasion of privacy, if you know what that means.

S: Well, we don't have to tell her you looked.

M: She'll find out. She'll know the minute she comes back. She's on a vacation, you know.

S: Oh, is she?

M: Sure. Granma told me. She won't be back for a while.

S: I see. Well, if she's gone, then she won't know you looked through her drawers and things, will she?

M: Oh, she'll know, all right. Mommy always knows. She knows everything. She can even tell when I'm lying. Right off. Did you know that? She's very smart.

S: But she won't know you looked if you're very careful. And also, if you find the letter, I'll buy you a nice present.

M: What will you buy me?

S: A doll, if you like.

M: I have a doll.

S: You can always use two dolls.

M: No, I can't. I have Dolly, and she's enough.

S: Well, what would you like?

M: Nothing.

S: There must be something you'd like.

M: Yes.

S: What?

M: A mink coat. Mommy always says she'd like one.

S: All right, I'll buy you a mink coat.

M: All right.

S: Will you look for the letter now?

M: No.

S: Well, why not? For God's sake . . .

M: Because I don't really want a mink coat. I don't really want anything. Besides, I'm very busy. I already told you, didn't I? I have to dress Dolly.

S: Monica . . .

M: You shouldn't shout. Mommy says it's impolite to shout, even on the telephone.

S: Monica, will you please . . .

M: I have to go now. G'bye. It was nice talking to you.

S: Monica!

M: What?

S: *Is* the letter in her desk?

M: I don't know.

S: Is it in her *room?*

M: I don't know. G'bye.

Carella looked up from his notes.

"Was that all?" he asked.

"Yes," Monica said. "I hung up. I had to dress Dolly. Besides, to tell you the truth, I was getting a little bored. I always get bored on the telephone, especially when I'm talking with grownups. All they want to know is how are you and have you been a good little girl. They never know how to talk. Only my friends know how to talk on the phone. I can dial Marjorie's number all by myself, did you know that? Would you like to see me dial Marjorie's number?"

"Not now," Mrs. Travail said.

"Did this person say he'd call back?" Kling asked.

"Well, I don't know if it was a *he,*" Monica said.

"Well, whoever . . . did he say he'd call back?"

"No. I just hung up."

"Did he call back?"

"No."

124

"Where is this letter, Monica?"

"I don't know. I think Mommy threw it out."

"Then why did you tell him . . . ?"

"Well, this person seemed so interested, I didn't have the heart to say Mommy'd thrown it out. Besides, I'm not so sure she did."

"Could we look through her room, Mrs. Travail?" Carella asked.

"Certainly," Mrs. Travail said.

"Mommy won't like it," Monica said ruefully.

"We'll be very careful," Carella said.

"Still. She won't like it. She's very fussy how her clothes are. Sometimes, when I play Red Cross Nurse and things, I use her scarfs for bandages. She takes a fit, she really does. She doesn't like her drawers all messed up. She's very fussy that way. You'd better be careful."

"We'll be very careful," Kling said.

"Do you think there's anything to this letter?" Mrs. Travail asked.

"The person who called Monica seems to think it's pretty important," Kling said. "As a matter of fact, your daughter thought so, too. Important enough to write and tell Ted Boone about it."

"She wrote to Theodore?" Mrs. Travail asked, interested.

"Yes." Kling paused. "Mrs. Travail, I thought you liked him."

"I do, immensely."

"Then why won't you release Monica?"

"Do *what?*" Monica asked.

"I don't think a child should live without a woman," Mrs. Travail said. "If he wants to take *both* of us in, I'll let her go tomorrow."

"I see. You said a while ago you didn't trust him."

"I don't. Not where it concerns Monica."

"Was Annie a drunkard, Mrs. Travail?"

"Certainly not!"

"Did you know that Mr. Boone was attempting to obtain legal custody by showing that Annie was a drunkard?"

"No. I didn't know that. But I'm not surprised. I love Theodore. But I'm afraid he would stop at nothing to get the child."

"Except murder," Carella said.

Mrs. Travail glanced quickly at Monica.

"We checked his alibi," Kling said. "You'll be happy to know he's in the clear."

"I told you that when first I talked to you," Mrs. Travail said.

"Who's this?" Monica asked. "Daddy?"

"Yes," Mrs. Travail said. "I love that boy. I wish he'd take us both in. I hate this. I hate legal battles and courts and everything that goes with it. But how else can I let him see which way is the right way? I hate distrusting him. I absolutely hate it."

"Well, he seems to have legal right to the child now."

"Maybe," Mrs. Travail said, and she shrugged. "What about this person who called Monica?"

"What about it?"

"The . . . the one who did it?"

"Possibly."

"Did what?" Monica asked.

"Nothing," Kling said.

"Is there any way of tracing the call that came?" Mrs. Travail asked.

"None whatever. Even if the party is still on the line, it's a pretty difficult thing to swing. Too much of the telephone company's equipment nowadays is automatic. If a call is made from a dial phone, it's impossible to trace. And if it's made from a phone without a dial—where you have to give the operator the number you're calling— it's *next* to impossible to trace. Sooner or later, the call gets circuited into the automatic system, and then you're lost in a maze of calls that could have originated anywhere. Police don't trace too many calls, Mrs. Travail. That's one of the popular fictions of crime detection."

"Well," she said, dubiously. "I suppose."

"Do you think we could look at Annie's room now?" Carella asked pleasantly.

Mrs. Travail smiled. "Of course," she said.

"This may take a little while," Carella said. "We want to do a thorough job.

So far, the killer was lucky.

They did a very thorough job—but they did not find the letter.

126

CHAPTER 14

THE BUREAU OF CRIMINAL IDENTIFICATION had dug out its packet on Charles Fetterick and sent it by messenger to the Detective Division of the 87th Precinct. In the cloistered silence of the squad room, Cotton Hawes studied Fetterick's card.

Hawes read through the card a second time, flipped it over to glance at Fetterick's fingerprints, and then leafed through the rest of the stuff in the packet. Fetterick had been released after he'd served his year's time. His last known address was 127 Boxer Lane in Riverhead, the building where they'd found him and then in turn lost him. The card didn't tell Hawes very much, except that Fetterick had tried to crack the safe of his employer. "Crack" it was perhaps an inaccurate term to use. He had tried to burgle it, and had come prepared with the combination to the safe.

Hawes looked at the I.B. card again.

Acton Photo-Engraving on Acton Drive in Riverhead.

He shrugged, told Meyer Meyer he was going out for a while, and then left the squad room.

Sam Kaplowitz was the owner of Acton Photo-Engraving. He was a giant of a man with a barrel chest and a black mustache that hung under his nose like a paint brush. "Sure, I remember Charlie," he said. "How could I forget Charlie? All my years in business, that was the first time I made a mistake. The *last* time, too, believe me."

"How long had he worked for you, Mr. Kaplowitz?" Hawes asked.

"Sam. Call me Sam."

"All right," Hawes said. "How long, Sam?"

"I should change my name, really. Not because I'm a Jew. This doesn't bother me. But Kaplowitz! Too long, isn't it? Also, it grates on my ears. When I hear it, it grates. I think I'll shorten it to Kaplan. Then everybody will know it's not because I'm Jewish I'm changing my name. I think it's important if you're Jewish you should be Jewish and not half-assish. That's the way I feel about it. How does Kaplan sound?"

"Pretty good," Hawes said.

IDENTIFICATION BUREAU

Name Charles Rudolph Fetterick

Identification Jacket Number R625621

Alias "Feathers" Fetterick, "The Bird," "Rudy the Bird."

Residence 8341 Paco Hill, Isola

Date of Birth May 5, 1935 Age 20

Birthplace Isola

Height 5'8" Weight 162 Hair Blond Eyes Brown

Complexion Sallow Occupation Engraver

Scars and Tattoos Appendectomy scar

Arrested by: Patrolman George Shapiro

"Kaplan," Klaplowitz said, testing the name. "Maybe I'll do it. I'll discuss it with my sons. It isn't that I would have to change the business name or anything. The business is named after the street we're on. Acton Drive. Could you imagine Kaplowitz Photo-Engraving? God, what a mouthful! I would choke every time I answered the phone."

"What about this boy, Mr. Kaplowitz?"

"Sam. Please."

"Sam."

Detective Division Number   29-1042-1955

Date of Arrest   6/21/55   Place   Acton Drive, Riverhead

Charge   Burglary

Brief Details of Crime   Fetterick, attempting to open safe of employer at Acton Photo-Engraving, was surprised at 1:07 A.M. by patrolman making rounds. He ran for exit clutching safe combination. Stopped when patrolman fired into the air.

Previous Record   None

Indicted   Criminal Courts, July 1, 1955

Final Charge   Burglary in third degree, Penal Law 404

Disposition   Sentenced not less than one year nor more than three Baily's Island.

"Thank you. I hired him. He was nineteen, I think. He didn't know anything, not a thing. I taught him. A nice boy. Charlie Fetterick. We used to call him Feathers. Or The Bird. Some of the boys in the shop called him The Bird. Friendly, you know. Nothing nasty intended. We taught him the business. In a year, he was a good engraver, believe me. A damn good engraver."

"What happened?"

"He decided to rob my safe. He didn't even have the right combination, do you know that? The slip of paper they found in his hand? The police? Well, it was the wrong combination. His lawyer tried to make a big thing out of that, tried to show he didn't intend to rob the safe. Some fun, he didn't. Argh, whattya gonna do? I trusted that boy. I liked him, too. But rob a safe? No. This I can't put up with. I was glad he went to jail. I'll tell you the truth, I was glad he went to jail."

"I don't blame you," Hawes said.

"I worked all my life, Mr. Hawes," Kaplowitz said. "I *still* got acid burns on my fingers from engraving. Still. After all these years. Nothing comes easy, nothing. Now I got my little business, but still nothing comes easy. This boy had a good opportunity. He learned a good trade here. So he wanted it the easy way. So he got prison, instead. Why do people have to do such things? Argh, I don't know. I just don't know." Kaplowitz blew his nose. "Is he in trouble again? Charlie?"

"Yes."

"What did he do? I heard he was out of prison last year. I'll tell you the truth, I was a little frightened. I thought he might bear a grudge, might come back to do some harm. Who knows what people who try to rob safes might do? Who knows?"

"But he didn't come back?"

"No."

"Not to apply for a job or anything?"

"No. Do you want to know something? I wouldn't have given him a job. I know that sounds terrible, but how many times can you get burned? I know a man is supposed to have paid his debt to society and all, but I wouldn't have given him a job if he came back here on his hands and knees and begged for it. I treated that boy like one of my

130

own sons. Thank God, my sons wouldn't try to rob my safe. What kind of trouble is he in?"

"He held up a liquor store and killed a cop."

Kaplowitz nodded somewhat sadly. "That's serious trouble. That I wouldn't wish on him. That's serious."

"Yes. It's very serious."

"It makes you wonder. Would he been in this trouble now if he hadn't been to prison? It makes you wonder."

"Don't wonder about it, Mr. Kaplowitz."

"Sam. Please."

"Sam."

"Still, it makes you wonder. You know, if there had been some *reason* for him to rob my safe, some good *reason*. If his mother was sick, or he needed the money very badly. But he was making a good salary here, and we gave him a big bonus at Christmas. No reason. No reason. A man like that, you can't feel pity. Still, I feel pity. I'm sorry he did wrong again. I'm sorry he got himself in such big trouble this time."

"Would you happen to know if he got a job anywhere in the field since his release from prison, Mr. Kaplowitz?"

"I don't know. I could check if you like. I know most of the other firms. I could check quietly. If you checked, it might scare him away. Do you want me to check around for you?"

"I'd appreciate it."

"I will. I don't like thieves, Mr. Hawes. I like honesty. Honesty is what should be in the world."

"Here's my card," Hawes said, handing it to him. "If you find out anything, please give me a call." Kaplowitz took the card and studied it.

"Cotton, huh?" he said.

"Yes."

"Mr. Hawes, when I go down to change my name, I'll give you a ring. We go together, okay?"

Hawes grinned. "Any time you're ready, Mr. Kaplowitz."

"Sam," Kaplowitz said. "Please."

The man who came into the squad room was holding his hat to his chest. He would one day be instrumental in solving a murder. His eyes were bloodshot, and his nose was running, and he had the disheveled look of a wino. He stood just outside the slatted rail divider. He didn't say a word. He stood and waited for someone to notice him. The first one to spot him was Miscolo, on his way from Clerical with a pot of coffee.

"Help you, Mac?" he asked.

"I wannuh . . . uh . . . is this . . . uh . . . this's the Detectives?"

"Yeah," Miscolo said. "What is it?" Standing close to the man, he could smell the cheap wine on his breath. He backed off a few feet. "What is it, Mac?"

"I wannuh . . . uh . . . I wannuh talk tuddy bull who's handlin' the . . . uh . . . the li'l girl got killed inny . . . uh . . . inny liquor store."

"Meyer!" Miscolo shouted. "Somebody to see you."

"Is that coffee?" Meyer said.

"Yeah."

"Bring it over." He walked to the slatted rail divider and watched Miscolo walk to his desk and pour a cup of coffee for him. He smelled the wine almost instantly, pinched his nostrils and released them, and then said, "Yup? What is it?"

"You . . . uh . . . workin' on the uh li'l girl who got killed inny liquor store?"

"I'm one of the cops working on it, yeah," Meyer said. "What is it? You kill her?"

"Me? Hey, me? Hey, no. Not me!" The man seemed about to leave. He put on his hat, and almost turned. Meyer's voice stopped him.

"I'm jokin', Mac. What is it?"

"Uh . . . George. You anny other one call me Mac. It's George."

"Okay, George. What is it?"

"Can I come inan siddown?"

"Sure. Come on in. You want a cup of coffee?"

"What is this?" Miscolo called over. "The Salvation Army?"

"Pour him a cup of coffee," Meyer said, grinning. "Break your heart, Miscolo."

"The Salvation Army," Miscolo muttered, but he poured a cup for the wino nonetheless. Meyer led him to the desk. He picked up his own cup, lifted it, and drank. The wino reached into his side pocket, pulled out a pint of cheap wine, uncapped it, and poured some into the coffee.

"First today," he said. He lifted his cup.

"What about the liquor store kill?" Meyer asked.

"Oh. Yeah. That."

"Yeah. What about it?"

"I seen it," George said.

Meyer put down his coffee cup. "You saw it."

"Um."

"The killing?"

"No. Not . . .uh . . . that. But I seen the rest."

"What rest?"

"The driving away."

"We always get the ones who see the driving-away,"
Meyer said. "How come you saw it?"

"I was . . . uh . . . layin' against the wall of the buildin'.
I was . . . uh . . . blind. Drunk, I mean."

"You don't mean to tell me you *drink!*" Meyer said.

"Uh . . . yeah. Occasionally. Now and then."

"Go ahead."

"I heard all the explosions. Terrible. And the noise of
bottles bustin'. Terrible. Uh . . . terrible."

"Go ahead."

"I . . . uh . . . leaned up on one elbow. This person ran
out of the shop and . . . uh . . . intera car. Drove away.
Whoom!"

"Man or woman?" Meyer asked.

"I dunno."

"Didn't you see?"

"No."

"You just saw this person get into a car and drive away,
is that right? But you can't tell me whether it was a man or
a woman."

"That's right. I was . . . uh . . . blind, you know? Ossi-
fied. Yeah."

"Did you happen to notice the license number?"

"Uh . . . no."

"Year of the car?"

"Uh . . . no."

"Make?"

"Uh . . . no."

"You just saw someone—either a man or a woman—
come out of the store and get into the car and drive away,
is that right?"

"Yeah."

"And that's all?"

"Yeah."

"Well, that's very helpful, George. Thanks a lot for coming up."

"Noddadall," George said.

He finished his coffee, put on his hat, and left the squad room.

Meyer sighed, and then looked at the brighter side of things. The person driving the car may have owned either a driver's license or a registered automobile. Unless he was an unlicensed driver driving a stolen car. In any case, the information was worthless at the moment.

Miscolo came over to Meyer's desk.

"How come your father visited you here?" he asked.

Meyer would not get angry. "Search me," he said. "I tell him to stay away, but he keeps coming. I guess he loves me. I'm hairy, but he loves me."

"Did you smell that guy?" Miscolo asked.

"My father?"

"Yeah."

"Sure."

"Pretty, huh?"

"Wonderful. I love that smell. It's my father's favorite cologne."

"He dresses neat, your Dad," Miscolo said.

"He always did. He almost took the best-dressed award away from Adolphe Menjou one year, would you believe it?"

"Sure, I believe it," Miscolo said. He sobered suddenly. "He give you anything?" he asked.

"Yeah," Meyer said. "A headache."

CHAPTER 15

THEY WERE running out of suspects and into dead ends.

They were running into airtight alibis and out of patience.

They were running up one-way alleys and phone bills.

They were running down a killer who did not yet exist.

They were running around in circles.

The man's name was Arthur Cordis. He was a teller in a bank. He had known Annie Boone and dated her. When the detectives walked in and asked to talk to him, he got a little nervous. He was scrupulously honest, but it didn't look nice for a pair of detectives to walk into a bank and ask to speak to you. It reflected on your honesty. He had never touched a dime in his life.

The detectives looked very tired. One was named Carella and the other was named Kling. Carella looked as friendly as a cobra. Kling looked as old as Elvis Presley. The three men walked to one of the managers' desks. It was all very embarrassing. Very embarrassing. It made Cordis feel like a criminal even though he had never touched a dime. Things made him feel like that. He always felt guilty whenever even a paper clip was missing, even though he hadn't been the one who'd taken it. He was just that kind of a man. Things made him feel like that.

"Mr. Cordis," Carella said, "we understand you were dating Annie Boone."

"Yes," Cordis said. "Yes." He wondered if they thought he had killed her. Certainly they could tell just by looking at him that he hadn't killed her! Did killers wear eyeglasses?

"When was the last time you dated her?" Kling asked.

135

"About . . . about a month ago. Yes. A month. You don't think I killed her, do you?"

"We're just asking some routine questions, Mr. Cordis," Carella said. He did not smile. God, he looked just like a cobra. He was the meanest-looking fellow Cordis had ever seen in his life. He wondered if he were married, and then he wondered what sort of a masochistic woman could marry a fellow like this Carella.

"Where'd you go that last time, Mr. Cordis?" Kling asked.

"The ballet," Cordis said. *"Swan Lake.* And . . . and *Pas de Deux.* And *Fancy Free.* The ballet."

"Where?"

"At the center."

"She like it?"

"Yes. Very much."

"Quiet girl?"

"Very refined."

"Ever see her shoot pool, Mr. Cordis?" Carella asked.

"I beg your pardon."

"Pool."

"That's what I thought . . . do you mean Annie? Annie Boone?"

"Yes."

"Shooting pool? Well, I should hardly think so. I mean, she simply wasn't that kind of a girl."

"Did you know she was divorced, Mr. Cordis?"

"Yes."

"Ever meet her daughter?"

"Monica? Yes."

"Ever talk to her on the telephone?"

"Who? Monica, do you mean?"

"Yes."

"I suppose so. Once or twice. Why?"

"Talk to her recently?"

"Why, no. Not since before the last time I saw Annie. Why?"

"Where were you on the night she was killed, Mr. Cordis?"

"That was Monday, June 10th. I remember," Cordis said. "I remember distinctly. I remember reading the papers the next day. I was shocked. Such a quiet girl. Refined, do you know? Refined. You don't meet that sort

136

of girl very much these days. Read a lot, too. Dreiser, and Thackeray and Balzac and Dostoevski. A big reader. I bought her 'A Fable' for Christmas."

"A fable? Which fable?"

" '*A* Fable,' " Cordis said. "Faulkner."

"Did she like it?"

"Loved it, I'm sure. A very nice girl. Splendid. A splendid girl. I was rather serious about her."

"And yet you hadn't seen her for a month, is that right?"

"Yes. That's exactly right. And that's exactly why I stopped seeing her for a while. Because I was getting so serious about her."

"I see."

"It makes you think, doesn't it, gentlemen? A wonderful girl like Annie. I stopped seeing her, and now she's dead, and now I'll never see her again."

"You still haven't told us where you were on the night of June 10th, Mr. Cordis," Carella said.

"You don't think I killed her, do you?"

"We'd like to know where you were that night, Mr. Cordis."

"I was at home."

"Alone?"

"No."

"Who with?"

"My mother."

"You live with your mother, do you?"

"Yes."

"Just the two of you home alone that night?"

"No. A neighbor-woman was in, too. We played gin together. My mother likes cards."

"Annie like cards?"

"I don't know. I never asked her."

"Were you ever intimate with her, Mr. Cordis?"

"How do you mean?"

"Well . . ."

"Oh! No, never. Why do you ask?"

"We just wanted to know."

"No, never. Well, I kissed her. Several times. Well, a few times, anyway. She wasn't that kind of a girl. You didn't take liberties with Annie. You just didn't."

"She ever mention a man named Jamie to you?"

"Jamie? I don't believe so. Is that for James?"

"We don't know."

"Jamie, Jamie . . . wait. Yes, she did. I recall now. I got rather angry. Well, not angry. That is . . ."

"Did you get angry, Mr. Cordis?"

"Yes. Well, as matter of fact, I did. She was out with me, and I didn't appreciate her discussing some other fellow. There is such a thing as courtesy. Not that Annie was ever discourteous. Never."

"Except this once," Carella said.

"Yes. Just this once. And I admit I got rather peeved. She seemed . . . well, she seemed rather fond of this Jamie, whoever he was."

"What did she say about him?"

"Only that she visited him in his flat, and that he was very charming."

"Did she say where the flat was?"

"Somewhere in Isola."

"Where in Isola?"

"She never said."

"What else did she say about Jamie?"

"Nothing that I can recall. Well, I told her I didn't think it was quite proper for an attractive young lady to go visiting a gentleman in his flat, and she sort of laughed."

"What did she say?"

"She said, 'Jamie's a darling. I adore him.' Something like that. Perhaps the intonation is wrong, but it was something like that. I got rather miffed. I repeated that I didn't think it was proper for her to see him in his flat."

"What did she say to that?"

"She said, 'Arthur, don't be ridiculous. I'm as safe with him as I am with you.' That's what she said." Cordis looked at Carella. "Is . . . ah . . . is something amusing?"

"No, no," Carella said. "Not at all. Go ahead."

"That's all there is to tell," Cordis said. "She never mentioned him again. I put off seeing her for a while because I was getting rather too fond of her. And then . . . then I read she was dead." Cordis looked at the desk top.

"And you were with your mother and a neighbor on the night she was killed, is that right?"

"Yes."

"From what time to what time?"

"From about seven-thirty to midnight."

"Leave the apartment all that while?"

"No."

"What was the neighbor's name?"

"Mrs. Alexander."

"Thank you, Mr. Cordis," Carella said, and he rose. Kling rose, too. Cordis remained seated.

"Is it all right? May I go back to my position now?"

"Sure," Carella said. "If you don't hear from us again, you can just forget we were ever here."

Arthur Cordis went back to his teller's cage. He never did hear from Carella and Kling again because, sure enough, he'd been playing cards on June 10th between 7:30 and 12 with his mother and Mrs. Alexander.

Mrs. Franklin Phelps did not seem surprised to see Meyer and Kling again. She opened the door for them, smiled and said, "Gentlemen, I was expecting you. Do come in."

The detectives followed her past the smoky mirror and into the period living room. They all sat.

"Why were you expecting us, Mrs. Phelps?" Meyer asked cordially.

"Because I figured it would occur to you sooner or later that I am a prime murder suspect."

"Well," Meyer said patiently, "we work rather slowly. We plod along, plod along."

"I'm delighted you're back," Mrs. Phelps said. "It gets lonely when Franklin's away."

"Mrs. Phelps," Meyer said, "we'd just like to check a few items."

"Yes?"

"You knew your husband was having an affair with Annie Boone, is that right?"

"Yes. And I knew he was paying her far more than she was worth at the shop. I knew all this, and I rather resented it, but I thought I'd wait until it blew over. These things do blow over, you know. That's what I told you. I am repeating that to you now. I did not kill Annie Boone. Let me set you straight on that at once."

"You have what is commonly known as a damn good motive, Mrs. Phelps."

"Yes." Mrs. Phelps smiled. "I haven't got the other two ingredients, though."

"What do you mean, Mrs. Phelps?"

"The means and the opportunity."

"You don't own a gun? Is that it?"

"No, I don't own one. Never have, never will. I detest guns. There isn't a weapon in this house, and there never will be one."

"You could have come across a gun, Mrs. Phelps. Guns aren't too difficult to come by these days."

Mrs. Phelps shrugged. "Granted. Perhaps I did. Perhaps I bought one—without showing the necessary pistol permit, which I do not own—but perhaps I did manage to buy one. Perhaps I paid a hockshop owner an exorbitant price in order to acquire a pistol. Perhaps I did. But what about opportunity, Detective Meyer? Isn't that important?"

"What about it, Mrs. Phelps?" Meyer said. "You tell us."

"Annie Boone was killed at the liquor store. That's a long way from where I was."

Meyer sighed patiently. "You drive, don't you, Mrs. Phelps?"

"Yes, I drive," she answered, smiling thinly. "But . . ."

"Then what was to stop you from . . ."

"But," she continued, "I could hardly have driven to the liquor store from Miami Beach. It's several thousand miles, isn't it? That's where I was on the night Annie Boone was killed."

"I see," Meyer said somewhat sourly.

"I suggest you call the Hotel Shalimar. Speak to the manager there. He will confirm the length of my stay, and he will also tell you that I was at a party given for the guests that night. He'll remember me. I'm good fun at a party. Call him." Mrs. Phelps smiled brightly. "Will that be all, gentlemen?"

The cop who spoke to the manager of the Shalimar on the long distance wire at the city's expense was Meyer Meyer.

"When did Mrs. Phelps check in?" he asked.

"On the 5th of June," the manager said.

"And when did she check out?"

"On the 14th."

"Did the hotel have a party on the night of June 10th?"

"June 10th? Let me see. Just a moment, please." There was an expensive pause. "Yes, June 10th. Yes indeed, we did."

"Was Mrs. Phelps at the party?"

140

"Yes, she was. A bright red dress. Very attractive."

"What time did she arrive?"

"The party started before dinner. It was for our guests, you understand. We're . . . well, rather famous for our cocktail parties."

"What time did it start?" Meyer asked.

"About four-thirty. In the afternoon."

"Uh-huh. And was Mrs. Phelps there when it started?"

"Yes."

"And what time did she leave the party?"

"Leave it? Why, I believe she was there all night."

"Are you sure?"

"Well, I'm not absolutely certain, of course. There were many women in red dresses. But I would say yes. Yes, I would say yes."

"What time did the party break up?"

"Well, it was a fairly lively party."

"What time?"

"We served breakfast at five-thirty," the manager said.

"What!"

"Yes."

"From four-thirty the previous afternoon?"

"Yes."

"It lasted all through the night? Until breakfast?"

"Well, yes. We're rather famous for our parties."

"You *ought* to be. Was Mrs. Phelps at breakfast?"

"Yes. Definitely. I remember serving her scrambled eggs myself."

"Still in the red dress?"

"Yes."

"And you think she was around all night, is that right?"

"We have thousands of guests," the manager said. "They flit in and out. There's a lot of drinking at these parties and . . . well, the management doesn't follow any of the guests' . . . activities too closely."

"I see," Meyer said. "Checked in on the 5th and out on the 14th, right? Was at your party on the 10th. Okay, sir, thank you."

"Not at all," the manager said, and he broke the connection.

Meyer sat morosely at his desk for a moment, and then decided to play a long shot. He called all the airlines and asked if round-trip passage had been booked from and to

141

Miami for a Mrs. Franklin Phelps on the night of June 10th, the night of Annie Boone's murder. And then, covering the pseudonym possibility, he asked if *any* woman had been booked for a round trip on that same night.

The airlines checked their flight records. The only passage they had given to Mrs. Phelps was on an early-morning flight to Miami on June 5th and a return flight on the 14th. Nor had any other woman made a round trip on the night of the 10th. Meyer thanked them and hung up.

Disgustedly, he belched. Long shots never paid off.

The cop who spoke to Monica Boone on the telephone was Bert Kling.

"Hi, honey," he said. "Know who this is?"

"No. Who?"

"Guess?"

"Tab Hunter?"

"Nope."

"Robert Wagner?"

"Nope."

"I'm not interested anymore," Monica said.

"Detective Kling," he said. "Bert."

"Oh, hello, Bert," Monica said warmly. "How are you?"

"Fine, thanks. Yourself?"

"Oh, just fine. I got second prize in school today."

"Really? What for?"

"Painting."

"That's wonderful. Honey, can I ask you something?"

"Sure."

"We already asked your grandmother this, but she didn't know. Maybe you would."

"What is it?"

"Your mother used to see a person named Jamie. Did she ever mention him to you?"

"Jamie?"

"Yes."

"Do you mean Jamison? Jamison Gray?"

"What was that name, Monica?"

"Jamison Gray. She told me all about him once. She said he was the sweetest saddest man in the whole world, and she said he was very kind and very gentle, and she said that someday she would take me to see him."

"You're not fooling me, are you, Monica?"

142

"No, not at all. Jamison Gray. Yes, that's his name. Is that the Jamie you mean?"

"Oh honey, I hope so," Kling said. "I certainly hope so. Thanks a lot."

"Bert?"

"Yes?"

"Do you know when Mommy's coming back from her vacation?"

Kling hesitated. "Uh . . . no, honey, I don't. I'm awfully sorry."

"I sure wish she'd hurry," Monica said.

"Yes."

"Well, I'll let you go," she said brightly. "You probably have lots of crooks and things to lock up."

"G'bye, Monica. Thanks again."

He hung up and lifted the Isola telephone directory from the bottom drawer of his desk.

"Anything?" Meyer asked.

"Maybe," Kling said. "Keep your fingers crossed. Gray, Jack . . . Gray, Jacqueline . . . Gray, James . . . Gray, James . . . Gray, James . . . oh my God, six of them . . . wait a minute, wait a minute! . . . here it is, Meyer! Jamison Gray! 1220 North 30th. Get your hat!"

"Hat?" Meyer said, running his hand over his bald pate. "I never wear a hat. Makes you lose your hair, don't you know?"

1220 North 30th was a clean-looking four-story brownstone. Meyer and Kling found a mailbox listing for Jamison Gray, and then climbed to the fourth floor of the building and knocked on the door of Apartment 44.

"Who is it?" a young voice asked.

"Open the door," Meyer answered.

"It's open," the voice said.

Kling, who was remembering Hawes' near fatal error, had his hand on the butt of his service revolver. Meyer snapped open the door standing to one side of it. There was no sound from within the apartment.

"Come in," the voice said.

His hand still on the gun, Kling peered around the doorframe. A boy of no more than twenty was sitting at the far end of the dark room, his face turned to the window.

From the doorway, Kling asked, "Jamie Gray?"

"Yes," the boy said. He wore black trousers and a white shirt open at the throat. His sleeves were rolled up over thin forearms. He did not turn from the window. He kept staring straight ahead of him, as if unaware there was anyone in the room with him.

"You know Annie Boone?" Kling asked.

"Yes," the boy said. He turned slightly from the window, but he looked at Meyer as if he thought he'd asked the question. "Did she send you?"

"No," Kling said. He blinked at the boy. The room was very dark. Except for the filtered shaftway light which came through the window, there was no illumination. He found it difficult to see the boy's features clearly.

"She didn't?" Gray asked.

"No."

"Oh," Gray said. "I thought she might have. She hasn't been to see me lately, so I thought maybe she sent a message or something." He turned back to the window. Kling and Meyer moved closer to him, into the room. The boy paid no attention to them.

"She come to see you often?" Meyer asked.

"Yes. Once a week, at least. It helped. She's a wonderful person."

"Ever take her out?"

"Once. We walked around the neighborhood. I don't feel like going out much."

"Where'd you meet, Gray?"

"In a bar. I don't know how. I went out one afternoon. I felt like having a glass of beer. Do you ever feel like that? Like having a glass of beer? Nothing tastes better than a glass of beer when you really feel like having one. She sat down at the table with me. Just like that."

"What'd she say?"

"She said 'What's *your* name?' I told her. I told her Jamie Gray. She was pretty drunk."

"Annie Boone?" Kling asked, surprised.

"Yes."

"Are you sure?"

"Certain. Her breath smelled terribly, and she was talking strangely. She was drunk. In fact, that's why she came up here with me. I asked her if she'd like a cup of coffee. She said 'Sure,' and we came back here."

"And after that, she kept visiting you, huh?"

144

"Yes. She came to talk. She said it was soothing."

"You live here alone, Gray?"

"Yes."

"What do you do for a living?"

"I used to be a pretty good piano player. I played with a band."

"What do you mean used to be? No more?"

"Well, I can still play. Naturally I can still play. What happened has nothing to do with my playing. But it's a little tough getting jobs. Going out and finding them, I mean. Besides, I don't much feel like it anymore."

"What do you mean?"

"Well, after what happened . . ."

"You mean what happened to Annie?"

"What?" Gray said, lifting his head.

"Do you own a gun, Gray?"

"What did you say about . . . ?"

"Do you own a gun?"

"No, of course not. What would I do with a gun? You said something about Annie. What . . . ?"

"Where were you on the night of June 10th, Gray?"

"I don't know. What difference does it make? You said . . ."

"Don't play dumb, Gray!"

"Dumb? Why? What happened on June 10th?"

"You've seen the newspapers, Gray! Come off it!"

"Newspapers? How could I . . . what is it? What are you trying to say?"

"Were you out of this apartment on June 10th?"

"I don't go out much at night. Or even during the day. Not since the acid . . ."

"Where were you on June 10th?" Meyer snapped. "Where were you on the night Annie Boone was killed?"

"Killed!" Gray screamed. He leaped out of the chair and whirled to face the two men. "Killed!" He stared at them blankly. "Killed! Killed!"

Kling's service revolver was already in his hand, pointing at Gray's midsection. Meyer stared at Gray, at the blank eyes in the old-young face.

"Put up the gun, Bert," he said softly. "He's blind."

CHAPTER 16

COTTON HAWES vindicated himself on the day they cap-
tured Charles Fetterick.

The call from Sam Kaplowitz came in at 8:27 A.M.
Hawes was summoned to the phone.

"Detective Hawes," he said.

"Mr. Hawes, this is Sam." He paused. "Kaplowitz."

"How are you, Mr. Kaplowitz?"

"Fine, thank you. I've located Charlie Fetterick."

"Where?" Hawes asked quickly.

"He's working for a place called Simpson Engraving.
That's in Riverhead."

"Are you sure?"

"Yes. From what Mr. Simpson told me, he's ready to fire
him. He hasn't been in to work for the last week or so."

"Thank you," Hawes said. "Mr. Kaplowitz, I want to get
on this right away. Thanks a million for calling."

"Don't mention it. Glad to be of assistance."

Hawes hung up. He looked up the number for Simpson
Engraving and called it. There was no answer. He had a
cup of coffee and tried again at 9:10. He spoke to a man
named Alec Simpson who said that Fetterick had been
working for him for six months. He was a good worker,
until just recently. Without calling in or anything, he'd
stayed away from work. It came as no surprise to Hawes
that the absenteeism had started on the day after Havilland's
death, the day after Fetterick had been wounded. He asked
if Simpson had an address for Fetterick. Simpson had two.
The one Fetterick had first used—his mother's apartment,
312 Bragin Street in Riverhead—and a later one, 127
Boxer Lane. Hawes jotted down the Bragin Street address,
thanked Simpson, took his service revolver from the top

drawer of his desk, and walked over to where Carella was typing.

"I've found Fetterick," he said. "Want to be in on the collar?"

"Think I'll get shot?" Carella asked.

Hawes smiled. "There's a chance," he said. "The help is sort of inexperienced."

"But maybe solid nonetheless," Carella said. He clipped his holstered gun into his back pocket. "Let's go."

They drove to Riverhead in silence. If either of the men felt any particular tension, neither showed it. When they reached 312 Bragin, they got out of the car silently and looked for Fetterick's name in the mailboxes. He was in Apartment 2A. They went upstairs quietly. This time, Hawes unholstered his gun before Carella did. This time, Hawes threw off the safety before Carella did. When they reached the apartment door, Carella stood to one side of it, and Hawes backed off for the kick. He hit the lock flatfooted, and the door sprang open.

The room was dead silent. They could see an easy chair and a corner of the bed from where they stood in the hallway.

"Out?" Hawes whispered.

"I guess," Carella said.

"Cover me."

Hawes stepped into the room cautiously.

The arm came from behind the open door. It looped itself around Hawes' throat and yanked him backwards. He was too surprised to flip Fetterick over his shoulder. He had only time to shout, "Steve! Get out!" before he felt the sharp snout of the automatic against his spine.

"Get in here, cop!" Fetterick said. "You run, and your pal is dead."

"Go, Steve!" Hawes said.

Carella came into the room.

"Drop the hardware," Fetterick said. "Both of you. Quick!"

Hawes dropped his gun. "Shoot, Steve," he said. "Drop him!"

"You do, and your pal's dead," Fetterick warned. "Drop the gun."

Carella dropped the .38.

"Inside," Fetterick said.

Carella moved away from the door, and Fetterick kicked it shut.

"Big cops," he said. "Saw you the minute you pulled up downstairs. Big cops."

"What now, Fetterick?" Carella asked.

"Big sons of bitches," Fetterick said. "Because of you bastards, I couldn't go to a doctor. I'm still carrying the slug, you bastards." He stood behind Hawes with the gun muzzle tight against Hawes' back. Carella moved across the room. "No funny stuff," Fetterick said. "One cop's already dead. A few more won't make it any worse."

"You've got it all wrong," Carella said. "You could get off with life."

"What *kind* of life? I done the prison bit already, thanks. I either get away clean this time, or I get the chair. That's the way I want it." He winced. The strain of keeping his arm around Hawes' neck was telling on his wounded shoulder. "Sons of bitches. Couldn't even go to a doctor," he said.

"Where's your mother, Fetterick?"

"Down getting something for breakfast. Leave her out of this."

"She's harboring a criminal."

"She doesn't know anything."

"She knows you're wounded."

"She doesn't know it's a gun wound. You got her on nothing. How'd you get to me? Was it the paint job on the car the first time?"

"Yes."

"I had to have it done. I thought it got spotted once. I couldn't chance it. What about now?"

"You shouldn't have looked for engraving work."

"Engraving's my work," Fetterick said.

"We thought burglary and robbery was," Hawes said snidely.

"Shut up!" Fetterick warned. Again, he pulled the gun back and then rammed it forward. Hawes felt the snout dig into his flesh. He braced himself.

"You guys don't have me tagged for this Annie Boone crap in the papers, do you?"

"*Was* it you?" Carella asked.

"No. I got an alibi a mile long. That's one thing you don't stick me with."

"Why don't you put up the gun like a good boy?" Carella asked.

"What for? So I get life on the state? Big deal. You guys walked into a coffin. You know that, don't you?"

"You're a stupid punk," Hawes said. "You wouldn't know how to . . ."

Fetterick pulled back the gun, ready to jab it into Hawes' back again. This time, Hawes was waiting for it. He moved quickly, twisting his body the moment the barrel left his back, twisting it inside the gun, throwing his weight at the same time so that he knocked the gun hand to one side, leaning forward simultaneously, his arms reaching up, his hands grabbing the arm that circled his neck.

The automatic in Fetterick's fist exploded, but Fetterick was in mid-air when it did, spiraling over Hawes' back. Carella was halfway across the room. Hawes threw Fetterick like a sack of flour. He landed on his back, sat up, and was bringing the automatic to bear when Carella kicked him. He kicked him in the arm, and the second shot went wild, and then Hawes took a flying leap, all one hundred and ninety pounds of him landing on Fetterick like a falling boulder. He pinioned Fetterick's arms and then began hitting him until he was senseless. Fetterick dropped the gun. He lay breathing heavily on the floor.

"That was a big chance," Carella said to Hawes.

"He was ready to shoot us," Hawes said.

"Yeah. Did I thank you?"

"No."

"Thanks," Carella said. "Let's drag this hunk of crap down to the car."

Charles Fetterick did not kill Annie Boone. His alibi for the night of June 10th was as solid as a rock. It didn't help Fetterick very much because the cops already had him on *one* murder. But, giving the devil his due, Fetterick did not kill Annie Boone.

CHAPTER 17

"WHO KILLED her?" they had asked at first.

And now they were asking something else again. Now they were asking, "Who was killed?" They had asked questions about a girl named Annie Boone, and they had learned that there were many girls named Annie Boone, and to know who had killed Annie they first had to discover which of the Annies had been killed. The vivacious redhead? The intellectual reader and ballet-goer? The poolshooter? The divorced wife? The mistress? The mother? The daughter? The social drinker? The drunkard? The girl who talked with a blind boy? Which was Annie? And which Annie had been killed? Or were they all Annie, and had the killer murdered someone who was all things to all men?

No, the killer had slain a specific Annie. And now the killer had a specific problem, and the problem was a letter.

Standing in the doorway across from the apartment house, the killer could watch everyone who went in or out of the building. When Monica and Mrs. Travail left the apartment, the killer crossed the street rapidly, and then went upstairs. It was not easy to force the door of the apartment. There could be no sudden sound, no sharp splintering of wood. And so the tool used was a simple wood chisel pried into the jamb, pressed, pressed with subtle force until the door sprang open. The killer went directly to the dead Annie Boone's room.

There, books were knocked from shelves, closets were ransacked, the record player was almost demolished, the bed was stripped, the mattress turned over—but the letter was not found.

The whirlwind swept destructively throughout the entire apartment, seeking, seeking, not finding, infuriated by failure, destroying property as senselessly as it had in the liquor shop on the night of the murder. The killer ransacked and destroyed and rampaged.

But the letter remained undiscovered.

The killer succeeded in doing two things.

First, the wild rampage brought the cops back to the apartment. This time, they realized just how important that letter was. This time, there were a dozen cops going over the place. This time, whenever two cops finished with a room, two other cops came in and started searching all over again.

They found the letter on Annie's desk.

She had tucked both letter and envelope into a larger envelope containing a brochure from one of the department stores. Safe within the pages of the brochure, the letter had escaped the killer's search. The killer, of course, did not have a dozen men searching, nor was a salary being paid for the solitary search.

The letter was very short. It was not a masterpiece of English composition. It said what it had to say. It was written in haste, but not in anger. It spoke of a murder which was coldly premeditated. It promised death in cold precise words. It said:

Annie Boone —
    Soon —
        You will know why.
You know why already.
You shall pay. Soon
and swiftly.
        You will die!

The killer had not bothered to sign the letter, but the

killer had signed two death warrants nonetheless: Annie
Boone's, and the killer's own. That was the second thing
the killer succeeded in doing.

The envelope was postmarked at International Airport at
8:00 A.M. on the morning of June 5th.

The rest was easy.

This is the stub torn from an automobile registration ap-
plication. This stub is on file in the Bureau of Motor
Vehicles in the state capital.

If you've ever registered an automobile, you signed the
stub. You signed your name. In your handwriting.

	Department of Taxation and Finance — Bureau of Motor Vehicles			
	1957	APP.	FEE $	
NOTE: See Instructions. On Reverse Side	**PASSENGER VEHICLE**			
1. PRINT Name of Owner............				
2. PRINT Residence............	City or Post Office and Zone No.........			
3. Employment or Business Address............	City or Post Office			
4. Date of Birth, if Individual Owner		**5.** Year and Make of Vehicle		
Month Day Year				
7. Cyls.	**8.** Color of Vehicle		**9.** Model No.	
11. Engine or Identification No.		**12.** Weight lbs.		**13.** Plate No.
14a. Have you ever been involved in a motor vehicle accident when you were not insured?		**b.** if yes, have you satisfied judgments resulting		
15. Is this vehicle to be used for hire to carry passengers or school children?		If "yes" state which		
16. You must submit proof of financial security with this application — Obtain Form company. (See instructions on other side.)				
I (We) the owner(s) of the above described vehicle certify that the vehicle is fully equi of the law and that the information given on this application is true.				

(Sign Name in Full—in Regular Handwriting)

(Do not write in this space)

MV 254A

Check B
☐ Individual owner
☐ Partner (See Reve
☐ Pres.   ☐ Vi
☐ Treas.   ☐ Se
☐ Lessee

This now is the reverse side of a stub torn from an ap-
plication for a driver's license. This stub, too, is on file in
the Bureau of Motor Vehicles in the state capital.

You signed it.

The first time you applied for a driver's license, you

signed the stub. There are stubs like this on file in the motor vehicle bureaus of almost every state in the union.

Not too long ago, a drunk named George had stumbled into the squad room of the 87th Precinct and said, "I wannuh . . . uh . . . I wannuh talk tuddy bull who's hadlin' the . . . uh . . . the li'l girl got killed inny . . . uh . . . inny liquor store."

He had spoken to Meyer Meyer, and then Miscolo had made a lot of bum jokes about the drunk being Meyer's father—but the drunk had told Meyer one thing, and maybe he was just an old drunk or maybe he was telling the truth, but he'd told Meyer that he'd seen someone *driving* away from the liquor store after hearing shots and breakage. If the drunk had been telling the truth, and unless the men of the 87th were up against the miracle of an unlicensed driver driving an unregistered car, the killer didn't have much time left.

There was the killer's handwriting on that letter mailed to Annie Boone. And there were thousands and thousands of signatures on the stubs in the Bureau of Motor Vehicles upstate. The comparisons began.

The drunk named George had not been lying, and the age of miracles was dead.

Mrs. Franklin Phelps sat quite regally in the straight-backed chair in the squad room. They let Steve Carella question her because Carella allegedly had a way with women, even though he was a married man. She knew it was all over, anyway. It was in her eyes and on her face. Anyone could have questioned her. A rookie off the streets could have questioned her.

"Mrs. Phelps," Carella said, "you left for Florida on the 5th, is that right?"

"Yes," Mrs. Phelps said.

"Did you mail this letter from International Airport before you boarded your plane?" He showed her the letter in its blue envelope.

"Yes," she said.

"You planned then to kill Annie Boone before you boarded that plane?"

"Yes," Mrs. Phelps said.

"Did you kill Annie Boone on the night of June 10th, Mrs. Phelps?"

Mrs. Phelps did not answer.

"Did you?"

"Yes."

"Do you want to tell us about it?"

"Why?" she said dully.

"We'd like to know."

"Go to hell," Mrs. Phelps said. "I killed the woman who was stealing my husband from me. I killed Franklin's mistress. I don't have to tell you anything else."

"You killed a lot more than a mistress," Carella said. "You killed a woman. In fact, you may not understand this, Mrs. Phelps, but you killed a lot of women, a lot of different women."

"I killed only one," she said. "My husband's mistress. That's the only one I set out to kill, and the only one I did kill."

She looked at Carella unblinkingly.

"Do you want to tell us about it?" he asked.

And again Mrs. Phelps said, "Go to hell."

The newspapers called it a crime of passion.

At the trial, the district attorney proved how coldly diabolical had been the murder plot conceived and executed by Mrs. Franklin Phelps. At the trial, she told how she had got the idea to kill Annie at the same time she'd got the idea for a vacation in Florida, and then explained how her mind had related the two, wedded them in a fatal plan. On June 5th, she had left for Miami. She could not resist sending the note from the airport, the note which led to her eventual capture. Her plan was a simple one. Even as she flew down to Miami for the first time, she had tickets for two other flights in her purse—one from Miami to this city under the name of Frieda Nelson; the other from this city to Miami under the name of June Arbuthnot.

On June 10th, the Hotel Shalimar had thrown a cocktail party. The party was a stroke of luck upon which Mrs. Phelps had not counted. She had planned to execute her scheme without benefit of any cover-plan, assuming her mere presence in Miami Beach at the time of a murder thousands of miles away would automatically eliminate her as a suspect. But since the party had presented itself, she used it. She appeared in her brightest red dress when the party started. She slipped away early and took a cab to Miami city and the airport where, as Frieda Nelson, she boarded a north-bound plane at 6:30 P.M. The plane landed at the International Airport here at 10:15 P.M.

Mrs. Phelps had gone to her car where she'd left it in the airport parking lot five days earlier. She drove to the liquor store, killed Annie with the .25 calibre automatic she had illegally purchased two weeks before in a hockshop, and then destroyed her husband's stock in a further attempt to divert suspicion from herself completely.

Forty minutes after the murder had been committed, she was back at the airport. As June Arbuthnot, she boarded the 12:30 A.M. south-bound flight to Miami. The flight enjoyed good weather all the way down, arriving in Miami at 4:00 A.M. She took a cab out to the beach and was back at the hotel in time for breakfast.

At the trial, despite the plea of guilty, the D.A. called Mrs. Phelps a "cold-blooded killer" and a "wanton murderess."

At the trial, Mrs. Phelps staunchly refused to divulge the name or location of the hockshop where she had purchased the .25.

At the trial, despite the D.A.'s roars for a death sentence, Mrs. Franklin Phelps was sentenced to life imprisonment.

The detectives from the 87th Squad were riding back from the trial in the police sedan after their stints as state's witnesses.

It was August, and it was hot, and the bulls rode in their shirt sleeves, Meyer on the front seat alongside Kling who was driving; Carella and Hawes in the back.

"You know who cracked this one?" Mcyer asked. "You think it was us?"

"It was Cotton Hawes," Kling said, smiling into the rear view mirror.

Hawes caught the smile and grinned back. "Sure, sure," he said.

"None of us," Meyer said. "Mrs. Phelps cracked it herself. Except she had help. She had help from a drunken wino named George. George is the hero of this piece."

Carella was strangely silent. Kling's eyes flicked from the thick traffic in the hot city streets to the rear view mirror.

"What's the matter, Steve?" he asked.

"Huh?" Carella said. "Oh, nothing."

"He's thinking of his wife," Meyer said. "It shakes a man to find out that wives are capable of homicide."

Carella smiled. "Something like that," he said.

"You afraid Teddy'll take a gun to somebody?" Kling asked. "Maybe I ought to stay away from marriage, huh?"

"No, no, that's not it. I was thinking of what Mrs. Phelps said to me. She said, '*I killed only one.*' Hell, maybe she didn't kill *any.*"

"That's not the way the D.A. read it," Hawes said.

"No. But maybe somebody else did the real killing, the *real* killing. Maybe somebody else took Annie Boone's life and, for all practical purposes, Mrs. Phelps' life, too. Maybe somebody killed them both."

"Who, Steve?" Kling asked.

"Franklin Phelps," Carella said. "If George is the hero of this piece, maybe Phelps is the villain. Maybe he's the rotten bastard in this kettle of fish."

156

"You mixed a metaphor," Hawes said.

The car went silent.

The men breathed the hot summer air. Slowly, the car threaded its way uptown to the precinct and the squad room.

6 classic mysteries starring Raymond Chandler's hard-boiled hero

Together with Dashiell Hammett, Chandler is credited as the inventor of the modern crime story. Here are savage, fast-moving stories of tough men and beautiful lost women in the tawdry neon wilderness of Southern California — by the master of detective fiction.

11

NE-10